THE DOLL
WITH
OPAL EYES

THE DOLL
WITH
OPAL EYES

JEAN DeWEESE

DOUBLEDAY & COMPANY, INC.
GARDEN CITY, NEW YORK
1976

All of the characters in this book are fictitious,
and any resemblance to actual persons, living or dead,
is purely coincidental.

ISBN: 0-385-11304-8
Library of Congress Catalog Card Number: 75-21222
Copyright © 1976 by GENE DEWEESE
All Rights Reserved
Printed in the United States of America
First Edition

FOR GINI ROGOWSKI,
DOLL EXPERT, VEGETABLE PROVIDER,
AND ALL-ROUND HELPFUL PERSON.

THE DOLL
WITH
OPAL EYES

As long as Roslyn Stratton could remember, the dream had been a part of her life.

It was always the same. First there were the forms, huge and indistinct, hovering over her, fading in and out of her vision as if seen through an impossibly thick, swirling fog.

Then there were the voices, senseless and relentless, pounding at her ears endlessly, engulfing her like a tide but saying nothing.

Then, in the midst of it all, began the struggle to breathe, the labored gasps necessary to suck in the ever-thickening, stifling air that seemed determined to smother her.

Then, as the struggle grew more desperate, as her lungs seemed to fill with the same unbreathable fog that surrounded her, the eyes would appear—eyes that glinted through the fog as it swirled around her, eyes that burned with an unearthly shimmering flame that seemed to be the most beautiful, the most important thing in Roslyn's life.

And finally—and this was what always brought her suddenly, shockingly awake—there was the wrenching ache that tore at her throat and erupted into a scream as the impossible, flaming eyes retreated and faded into the surrounding mist—and were gone.

CHAPTER 1

Fowler's Main Street, deserted in the late evening rain, was barely recognizable as the same street Roslyn had driven along on a sunny afternoon less than a week before. The same stores lined the street, but now they were darkened and vacant, peering at her forlornly through the veil of rain. The only motion was in the reflection of her own headlights as they darted from window to window, following her erratically along the far side of the sidewalk. A lone car, angle-parked against the curb in the middle of the three-block business section, seemed lost and abandoned. The gray, stone castle that passed for the Barton County Courthouse still stood at the center of the town square, guarded by the inevitable Civil War cannons and stone lions. The week before, in the sunlight, the courthouse had seemed quaintly medieval, but now, its upper towers visible only as shadows in the watery darkness, it was forbidding and ominous and only deepened the feeling of depression that had been growing steadily in Roslyn ever since the rain had begun more than a hundred miles earlier.

She knew, of course, what was causing the depression, just as it had caused dozens of others over the past six years. The knowledge did not, as so many amateur psychologists in college had insisted it should, ward off the depressions. If anything, the knowledge deepened the mood, giving her mind something to focus on.

It had been on another night much like this one that the sheriff had come to their door. The rain had been falling steadily, drearily, without even the small bit of brightness and relief that lightning would have provided, when Roslyn's mother had gone to answer the insistent knocking. Roslyn, awakened from a light sleep, had come to the door of her own room to peer through the crack, watching curiously as her mother opened the front door.

"Alicia Stratton?"

The sheriff, his hooded raincoat half concealing his face, stood outside the screen door on the small front porch.

"Yes? What can I— You're Sheriff Wilson, aren't you?"

"That's right, Mrs. Stratton. Could I come in for a minute?"

Her mother had hesitated as she looked up into the sheriff's face uncertainly, then stepped back. Water dripping from his raincoat, he stepped inside just enough to allow the door to close behind him. His eyes, Roslyn remembered, had looked everywhere except at her mother's face.

"Yes, Sheriff, what can I do for you?" It may have been Roslyn's imagination—or merely a time-induced distortion of the memory itself—but it seemed that her mother's voice was unsteady, as if she already anticipated what the sheriff was struggling to say.

"Mr. Stratton—Thomas Stratton—is your husband?"

She nodded, and now Roslyn was positive that her mother had blinked nervously.

Then the words, low and uninflected, Sheriff Wilson's lips barely moving as he spoke: "There's been an accident."

There had been no hysterics. Perhaps, Roslyn often thought, it would have been better if there had been. Perhaps, if she and her mother had broken down into screaming tears, that would have gotten rid of it then and there. Perhaps an explosive release at the first news would have eliminated all the subsequent periods of gloom that descended—on Roslyn, at least—nearly every time that—

Roslyn shook her head sharply until she could feel the nearly straight, black hair that framed her angular face slapping at her cheeks and forehead. Nervously, she ran the fingers of her free hand through the medium-short hair, still tangled from the hours of open-window driving before the rain had started.

"Enough!" She spoke the word aloud, harshly, directing it half at herself, half at the rain that still held its own against the sluggish windshield wipers. Her voice was startlingly loud in the interior of the aging Rambler, and it brought a brief smile to the corners of her wide, full-lipped mouth.

Suddenly, she felt better, and she wondered if, finally, she was beginning to get the better of these somber moods. She certainly should be, after six years. And a pointless mood of depression was one of the last things in the world that she needed now. She was more than four hundred miles from home, and in less than twelve hours she would be starting her first job since graduating from college nearly three months before. A job she intended to stay with for at least a few years, so she didn't want the very first day blighted by—by whatever it was that forced such moods on her.

She shook her head again and forced herself to concentrate on the street ahead. She squinted through the windshield, wishing that the wiper blades were a little faster and less streaky. The only street sign she could locate was on the opposite side of the intersection she was approaching, out of range of the headlights. The street she wanted to turn on, she knew, couldn't be far from here, but she couldn't remember if it had been two or three blocks south of the last stoplight of the business section. And it all looked so different now. The buildings all seemed to take on the same monotonous gloom that had hovered over the courthouse, and she couldn't remember if she had seen them before or not.

Further down the street, a light caught her eye. A service station? As she drew closer, a brightly lighted "Gas For Less" sign came into view next to the sidewalk. Perched on top of the tiny, glass-enclosed building behind the pumps was a second sign, this one loudly proclaiming the station's name: Heyde's.

Another smile pulled at Roslyn's lips. Yes, this was the street she wanted, Twelfth Street, just beyond "Heyde's" service station. She could hardly forget a name like Heyde, not after it had, the week before, conjured up in Roslyn's mind the image of a little Swiss girl with pigtails, dutifully pumping gas as she bitterly complained about how everyone misspelled her name. It was not, Roslyn admitted ruefully to herself, high humor, but it was certainly an improvement over the gloom that had dominated the last hundred miles.

As she slowed and made the left turn onto Twelfth, she saw a young man seated inside the station, seemingly oblivious to the outside world, his feet propped up on a battered desk, a crushed paperback in one hand. One of the Heydes, she wondered idly as she completed the turn? Very disappointing. No pigtails.

Twelfth was considerably narrower than Main, and the occasional cars parked on either side narrowed it still further, and Roslyn returned her full attention to driving. After a half dozen blocks, the street crossed a railroad track, moved past a darkened, deserted factory set well back from the street, and then curved off to the left, leaving the town and its occasional street lights behind.

After a half mile, the road curved back to the right. A few hundred yards beyond the curve, a light glowed dimly through the still-falling rain.

Involuntarily, Roslyn pressed down on the accelerator, and in a few moments she was turning into a narrow, gravel drive and parking at the edge of a large, oval turnaround area a hundred feet back from the road. Two other cars, neither of them quite as old as her own ancient Rambler, were already there. Vivian's and her father's, she assumed. A bare bulb on top of a ten-foot-high pole cast a harsh light over the entire area. Beyond the turnaround was a sagging, abandoned barn and a couple of equally dilapidated sheds. To the left of the drive, a dozen yards away, was a two-story frame house.

Even before Roslyn turned the engine off, the back door of the house flew open and her cousin Vivian Jefferson, a sweater pulled loosely over a plain, utilitarian-looking blouse and slacks, a large, black umbrella held high, hurried along the series of small flagstones set into the ground to form a walkway. She stopped next to the car, her free hand on the handle of Roslyn's door.

"Just leave your bags out here," she said as Roslyn swung the door open and slid her long legs out of the car. "We can get them after this frightful deluge lets up."

Vivian held the umbrella out so that barely a drop of rain touched anything but the flared cuffs of Roslyn's burnt-orange pantsuit—her one real extravagance since graduating—as she maneuvered the rest of the way out of the car and stood up.

Vivian's smile was almost eager as she raised the umbrella to accommodate Roslyn's five-feet-nine, but Roslyn, who had always felt a little gawky because of her height, hastily ducked down to bring herself closer to Vivian's barely more than five feet. Clustered together, Roslyn's arm slipping hurriedly across Vivian's shoulders, the two of them half walked and half ran the dozen yards to the back door of the house.

After a clumsy moment of untangling themselves and getting the umbrella lowered, Roslyn followed Vivian through a small service porch and into the kitchen, brightly lighted by a pair of overhead fluorescent tubes. Vivian stood the loosely folded umbrella on a spread-out newspaper in the corner and quickly turned back to Roslyn. Vivian's rounded face, so different from Roslyn's almost square one, reminded Roslyn of the old pictures she had seen of her own mother. Faintly flushed after the dash in from the car, Vivian ran a hand nervously through her short-cropped, reddish-blond hair as she spoke.

"Welcome to Fowler," she said, the words coming rapidly, "and don't think the weather is always this bad. It's the first rain we've had in a month, and the farmers were— But that doesn't mean anything to you, does it? Look, you must be exhausted from all that driving. Here, sit down."

Vivian touched one of the straight-backed chairs by the kitchen table, then spun around and, in two steps, was at the electric range. "I have some coffee all ready for us. I— You do drink coffee, don't you?"

Roslyn nodded, smiling. "Yes, more than I should, but—"

"I know. So do I, and I often wonder if I really like the stuff."

Vivian picked up the glass percolator from its place on the range and filled two cups that were already sitting on the table.

"But I keep right on," she continued, still talking quickly, nervously, "nothing stops me." She set the percolator back on the stove and returned to the table. "Now come, sit down. Take it easy for a few minutes—and tell me about your job. You didn't have much time to talk last week."

Roslyn grinned, almost laughing. She had always thought that she herself tended to rattle on endlessly when she was nervous, but she could see that she had nothing on Cousin Vivian.

"There's not much to tell, yet," Roslyn said. Oddly, Vivian's very nervousness seemed to be having a calming effect on Roslyn, as if her subconscious was trying to be perverse. Or maybe it was just the tiredness and stiffness. She pulled in a deep breath, almost like the beginning of a yawn, and stretched her long arms out sideways and moved her shoulders and head back and forth, trying to work out some of the stiffness that had accumulated over the past nine hours. "And as for sitting down, after four hundred miles in that ten-year-old clunker of mine, I'm not sure I ever want to sit down again. Still . . ." She looked down at the chair, leaning against it for a moment. "Still, as long as I don't have to drive it anywhere, I suppose it's all right."

Taking her time, Roslyn moved around the chair and lowered herself onto it, propping her elbows on the table, bracketing the coffee cup in front of her. She sat silently, letting the aroma float up and swirl around her face, letting her mind drift aimlessly.

Vivian sat down opposite her and picked up her own cup but did not sip any of the coffee. "Come on, Roslyn," she said after a few seconds, "are you going to tell me about it? How did you ever find out about it?"

Roslyn blinked, coming sharply out of her reverie. "Find out? About what?"

"The job, of course. I mean, you're two states away, and I hadn't even heard about an opening here myself."

"Oh, that's simple enough. The placement office at school. They get notices from libraries all over the Midwest and they pass them on to the recent graduates."

"And the job? What will you be doing?"

"Nothing spectacular, I'm sure. Someone donated enough money to the Fowler library for them to buy a bookmobile, and they had to hire another librarian to take care of it. I'll spend at least part of my time on it, going around to all the country schools. Other than that . . ." Roslyn shrugged lightly. "Come in and see sometime. We're always looking for new customers."

Vivian looked doubtful. "But why here? There must be jobs for librarians in more exciting places than Fowler."

"Perhaps. But jobs aren't that plentiful at the present, particularly for someone with a brand new library science degree and no experience. Besides, in a way, Fowler is my home town."

But even as she spoke, a part of Roslyn's mind wondered: Why *did* I come here? There were other openings I could have applied for, openings that were both closer to home and in larger cities. Saying it was her "home town" was, she knew, nonsense, for she remembered nothing of the town. She had left—her parents had left —when she had been less than a year old, and they had never been back, not even for a visit.

And yet, she had come.

She looked up to see Vivian smiling at her, still a little nervously.

"Whatever your reason," Vivian was saying, "I'm glad you're here. And to tell the truth, I hope you don't find an apartment right away and have to stay with us for a good long time."

"Don't be too sure about that," Roslyn warned. "But I don't think there'll be much of a problem finding a place. Mrs. Sutherland, at the library, said there were always several good apartments available in Fowler. Incidentally, there's one thing I have to do before I get too comfortable here—I have to phone my mother. She'll be getting frantic if she doesn't hear from me pretty soon. I can get the charges from the operator so I can pay for the call, of course, and—"

"Don't be silly! You don't have to pay for anything, least of all a phone call. And the phone is right in here."

Vivian had gotten up and moved past the electric range to the entrance to a small alcove. A phone was on the wall in the alcove, and three or four bookshelves, filled mostly with cookbooks, took up the space below the phone.

Roslyn followed Vivian to the alcove, and Vivian indicated a chain that dangled from a small plastic light fixture hanging from the ceiling.

"I have to dial in the dark a lot," Vivian said, holding her hand as high over her head as it would go, still a good two inches below the end of the chain. She stepped back and Roslyn reached up and easily pulled the chain, flooding the area with light from the single bulb that swayed back and forth from the pull.

As she took the receiver down, Roslyn started to ask why no one had ever lengthened the chain, but Vivian had already rushed in with another question, this one about Roslyn's mother.

"She's her usual self," Roslyn said absently, as she completed dialing and waited for the series of clicks and clunks that indicated the long distance call was going through. The receiver at the other end was picked up before even the first ring was completed, and Roslyn barely suppressed a chuckle as her mother's anxious voice came over the line. She must have been camping next to the phone, waiting to pounce on it the instant it rang.

"Roslyn? Is that you?"

"Yes, Mother, it's me."

There was a moment's silence and then an audible sigh. "You're all right? Where are you calling from?"

"Yes, I'm fine, just a little tired. It's a long drive. And I'm calling from Carl's house."

"Carl's, yes. I *was* getting a little worried, you know. I thought you were planning to get there earlier than this."

"I was, Mother, but I ran into some bad weather, and—"

"Bad weather? What? What was it?"

"Just rain, Mother, nothing to worry about. It was pretty heavy, though, so I had to take it a little slower the last hundred miles."

A hesitation. "You're all right, then? Everything's all right?"

"Yes, Mother, everything is just fine. Fowler is still here, even after all these years and a hard rain."

"Well, I know *that!*" There was a touch of petulance in the voice. "But you know how I worry."

"I know, but everything is perfectly all right. And before you ask—yes, I did get something to eat, so you don't have to worry about my starving, either."

"I'm very glad to hear it, Roslyn, very glad. And you didn't have any trouble with your car?"

"No, Mother, no trouble, and—" She stopped. She had been about to say that the lack of trouble itself had been a surprise, but she realized it would be a mistake.

"Yes?" her mother asked a moment later. "You were going to say something else?"

"Something else? No, nothing more. I was just saying I didn't have any trouble with the car, or with anything else."

"That's good." A pause. "By the way, how is Carl these days?"

"I couldn't say, not yet. I haven't talked to him."

"But—isn't he home?"

"I think he is, but I thought I'd better call you first thing, before you had time to really get yourself worked up. Would you like to talk to him? He's probably—"

"No," her mother said quickly, "that won't be necessary. I was just curious. And Vivian? Is she all right?"

"She's fine, too, Mother, and she's standing right here, if you—"

"No, thank you, I—" She broke off and the line was silent. After several seconds, her voice returned. "I'm glad you called. And you *will* let me know if there's anything I can do, anything at all that you need."

"Yes, Mother, I will. And as soon as I find an apartment, you'll have to come to visit me. It shouldn't be too long. I understand apartments are quite plentiful."

"Yes, that would be nice," her mother said, but her voice sounded uncertain now. "Do you think you'll be coming back home one of these days?"

Roslyn laughed suddenly. "Mother! I just arrived a few minutes ago! I haven't even started my new job or unpacked my bags, and—" She paused, shaking her head, still half laughing and looking toward Vivian, who was standing just beyond the telephone alcove looking puzzled. "Look, Mother, I'll have an apartment in a few days, so you just plan on coming down here for at least a weekend, maybe even as soon as next Saturday. If I get something by then, I'll call you again."

"I don't know if—"

"Don't worry about it, Mother! If you want some time off at the store, I'm sure Joe will give it to you. You've worked there ever since—for the last six years. Joe will give you as much time off as you want. But look, Mother, I'd better hang up before we run Carl's phone bill completely out of sight."

Vivian was making "don't-worry-about-it" gestures, but Roslyn shook her head and went on. "For the tenth time, Mother, I'm all right. And I'll let you know as soon as I get a place of my own so you can come down for a visit. For right now, unless you want to talk to Carl or Vivian . . ."

She waited a second for a reply, and when there was none, concluded: "I'll be in touch with you in a few days, Mother. Good-by."

She held the receiver a moment, heard a distant "Good-by, Roslyn," and hung up. She turned to Vivian, who had been looking puzzled during the later exchanges, shook her head, and moved back into the kitchen.

"Mother got it in her head," Roslyn said as she sat down at the table again, "that I shouldn't come to Fowler, and she's been fretting about it since I first mentioned it last week."

Vivian frowned puzzledly. "But why?"

"I don't know, Viv, I have no idea." Roslyn picked up her coffee, now cool enough to sip easily. "I think she's just upset about my moving so far away, but she won't admit it. Although I have to admit she's been acting a little strangely ever since I mentioned the job."

A shadow seemed to settle across Vivian's face as Roslyn spoke. "You're probably right," Vivian said, smiling ruefully. "Parents are like that. I think Father would have a fit if I ever tried to move away from Fowler."

Roslyn started to answer quickly but then hesitated. She was, after all, a guest in their house, and she could hardly advise Vivian to let her father have the fit if that's what he wanted to do. From the occasional letters she had gotten from Vivian—one every few months—it had been easy enough to read between the lines and see that, no matter what Vivian said, her father was somehow conning her into continuing to live at home and be, to all intents and purposes, his housekeeper. Roslyn also strongly suspected that Vivian's father had been responsible for the sudden departures of at least a couple of men that Vivian had been seeing.

"Perhaps," Roslyn said finally, noncommittally. "But I never thought Mother would be that way. There was no problem at all when I was away at school."

"But that wasn't nearly so far—or so permanent."

"I suppose that's true, but still . . ." Roslyn shrugged and took another sip of the coffee. She looked around. "By the way, where *is* your father?"

Vivian glanced at the clock that hung from the wall above the refrigerator. "Probably engrossed in the ten o'clock news. He never misses it, even on Sunday."

Roslyn looked toward the door leading to the rest of the house. Listening carefully, she could make out the murmur of a voice in the background. The ten o'clock news, she assumed.

"Look, Vivian," she said, turning back to her cousin, "are you *sure* this is all right? My staying here like this? Are you sure your father doesn't mind? After all, just because I'm a niece doesn't mean he automatically has to give me a place to stay while I'm hunting for an apartment. It's not as if we had been keeping in touch all these years. I mean, except for those occasional letters between you and me, we're complete strangers, and—"

"Don't be silly, Roslyn! Of course it's all right. Why on earth wouldn't it be? We live all alone here, with more room than we know what to do with. Why—" Vivian stopped, her eyes downcast a moment. "Why, I don't see why you couldn't just stay here permanently. If you wanted to, of course."

Roslyn was taken aback by the sudden invitation and the obvious eagerness with which it was given.

"Thank you," she said, a little uncertainly, "but I couldn't, really. Besides, it's a little early for you to be giving me any long range invitations. I've only been here a few minutes. By the end of the week, if I'm here that long, you'll probably be more than ready to throw me out."

Vivian shook her head emphatically. "No, I wouldn't! It would be nice to have someone around besides Father."

"Don't be too sure," Roslyn said lightly, and then, partly to avoid any further invitations, she got up and went to one of the kitchen windows, pushed the curtain back and looked out.

"Looks like your frightful deluge is slacking off," she said. "I had better take advantage of it to get my bags." She leaned closer to the window, shading her eyes against the reflected light. Outside, the naked bulb on the post was still on, and Roslyn could see occasional drops of rain spattering on the flagstones that led back to the cars, but that was all. It was coming down much more lightly than before.

"It's probably as dry as it's going to get," she said, as she turned to get her purse from the table and extract her keys.

She had them in her hands and was reaching for the back door when a new voice startled her.

"Well, Roslyn Stratton, I presume. It's nice to see you—at last. And how's Sister Alicia these days?"

Roslyn turned. A stocky man, an inch or two shorter than Roslyn, stood in the doorway leading to the rest of the house. He looked to be in his fifties; a salt-and-pepper crew cut topped a face that, despite its roundness—like her mother, Roslyn thought, startled at the resemblance—appeared hard and rugged.

"Nice to see you, too, Mr. Jefferson," Roslyn said formally, the name sounding stiff and stilted even as she spoke it. But somehow she could not bring herself to call this stranger "Uncle Carl."

"And my sister? How is Alicia Stratton these days?"

"Mother is just fine. I was talking to her a few minutes ago, letting her know I arrived safely. She likes to worry about me, even if I am over twenty-one."

"I can understand that," he said, glancing briefly toward Vivian, then toward one of the windows. "We had better get your bags before it starts raining again. I was just watching the weather on TV, and according to them, the rain will keep up most of the night. This letup probably won't last long. Here, give me your keys and I'll get your stuff."

"No, that's all right," Roslyn protested, uncomfortable at the thought of someone having to go out of his way for her. "I can get—"

Carl Jefferson laughed, glancing toward his daughter. "All right, Roslyn Stratton," he said, his eyes returning to Roslyn, "we'll both get them. All right?"

Without waiting for a reply, he pushed open the door and started across the service porch. Roslyn followed closely, hurrying to keep up. The rain seemed to pick up as she struggled with the trunk lock, and she could feel the drops hitting her back and quickly soaking through her light blouse. Hurriedly she lifted the lid and scooped out two of the smaller bags.

"That big one," she said, pointing as she straightened up, "that's the only one I really need for tonight. Just leave the rest."

Jefferson grabbed up the indicated bag plus one more and slammed the trunk lid shut. He reached the back door of the house almost on Roslyn's heels as the rain began coming down in full force once again.

"Just made it," he said, as they moved into the kitchen. "It's really coming down again. Looks like they were right on TV after all."

"Did you get everything you need?" Vivian asked. "If you need anything else, you're more than welcome to mine."

"I have more than enough for the time being," Roslyn assured her, "but thanks just the same."

"Come on, Roslyn Stratton," Jefferson said, motioning for her to follow him, "I'll show you to your room. You've got the one next to Vivian's."

He led the way out of the kitchen, past the telephone alcove, into the hall and up the stairs. Vivian followed a few steps behind Roslyn. At the top of the stairs, Jefferson turned to the left and pushed open a door near the end of the short hall.

"Vivian is just next door," he said, nodding to another door just to the right, "and I'm down the hall at the other end. Think this will do you all right?"

"I'm sure it will," Roslyn said, looking around the room. It was small but well decorated, and Roslyn noticed that the curtains looked stiff and starchy, as if they had just been put up. The bureau against one wall looked spotless and polished. The bed itself, a spacious double with a gold spread, was made to perfection, not a wrinkle or even a dent showing in the smooth surface. Jefferson dropped the two suitcases on the bed and stood back. Vivian remained just outside the door, watching quietly.

"Viv's been fussing with it all weekend," Jefferson said, glancing toward his daughter. "I told her she shouldn't make such a fuss, but she seemed to get a charge out of it."

"Really, you shouldn't have gone to all that trouble," Roslyn said, most sincerely, almost wishing she hadn't given in to the impulse to get in touch with Vivian the week before.

"It's very nice," she went on, covering Vivian's protests that it had been no trouble at all. "I just hope I haven't caused you too much trouble, either of you. It was just an impulse to call you when I did, after they told me I had the job. I didn't intend to invite myself to live here. I really didn't."

Jefferson smiled. "I know you didn't. Viv told me she practically had to twist your arm to get you to accept. But after all, you are my sister's daughter, and it's the least we can do while you're getting settled."

"I appreciate it," Roslyn said, looking toward Vivian and back to her father. "But I don't—"

"Not another word," he said. "You're Alicia's daughter, and you're entirely welcome. I only wish that you—and your mother—could have visited before. Why, the last time I saw you, you were just a baby, not even a year old. That must have been—how long? Twenty years ago?"

"At least twenty-one," Roslyn said, still feeling vaguely uncomfortable and something like an intruder despite their protests. "I'm twenty-two now."

"Yes, well, you'll have to tell me all about your mother, how she's been getting along since—" He hesitated, and when he spoke again, though his expression remained pleasant, his voice seemed different, harder. "I thought maybe, after your father died, your mother might have come back. Even if it was just for a visit."

Before Jefferson could say more, Vivian got her courage up and moved quickly past him to stand next to Roslyn.

"I'm sure Roslyn will be happy to tell you whatever you want to know, Father—after she's gotten unpacked. It will take all night for the wrinkles to hang out of her clothes as it is, without letting them sit in those suitcases any longer, while you get her to tell you her life story. Now you just go back downstairs, out of the way, and I'll help her unpack and get things hung up."

Jefferson hesitated, looking from Roslyn to Vivian. Again, his features remained fixed and pleasant, but his eyes . . . He shrugged lightly.

"Of course," he said, and there was a distant quality in his voice. "I wasn't thinking. There will be plenty of time to catch up on family history, now that you're here. And I'm sure you're exhausted after all that driving—and Viv tells me that you have to be at the library bright and early in the morning, too. I'll just leave you alone for the moment, you and Vivian."

He turned to the door, stopping just outside. "But this doesn't mean that you're getting off scot-free, Roslyn Stratton. I have a lot of catching up to do. The last twenty-one years of my sister's life . . ."

Still he was smiling, but his tone shifted again and the hardness was unmistakable.

"Until tomorrow, then . . ." And he was gone.

CHAPTER 2

Roslyn was feeling more her normal self Monday morning. In the first place, when Vivian had finally said good night after nearly an hour of chatting, and Roslyn had, more out of nervous habit than anything else, turned on the tiny portable TV set in her room, there had appeared the familiar and hairy face of Lon Chaney, Jr., only minutes away from one of his many werewolfly deaths, this one at the hands of the Frankenstein monster, who was at the time strapped to the next table, snarling unhappily. Roslyn had put the TV set on the bed and settled in under the covers as with an old friend, and the next thing she knew, it was 2 A.M. and a blank and fuzzy screen was hissing quietly at her in the darkness.

Then, in the morning, she found that the wrinkles had hung out of her blue pantsuit better than she had ever expected, and to top it off, breakfast—prepared by an incredibly early-rising Vivian—was excellent. Roslyn even managed to satisfy Carl Jefferson's pointed curiosity about her parents without any major problems.

All in all, things were looking up considerably as she set out on the short drive into Fowler shortly after eight. Except for roadside puddles, all traces of the rain were gone, and except for a few high, fast-moving clouds, the sky was a crisp blue. A dry breeze ruffled the trees, and even the Rambler seemed to be running better than it had in several months.

The city of Fowler was again alive, dozens of cars already lining the downtown streets, and the Barton County Courthouse once again appeared only quaint and medieval. The morning sun glinted off the dozens of windows, giving them a sparkling life of their own, and the inevitable pigeons swooped and darted and cooed around the towers that had seemed so ominous less than twelve hours earlier.

The library, a block west of the courthouse, was a square, blocky building made mostly of brick and stone. In the back, just off the alley, were a half dozen narrow, gravel parking spots, and Roslyn pulled into the end one. The bookmobile, a huge, dark blue bus, sat by the curb next to the alley, and Roslyn remembered what Mrs. Sutherland, the head librarian, had said to her last week.

"Unfortunately, the donation that allowed us to purchase the bookmobile didn't allow us to also build a shelter of any kind. As a result, it sits out in the street all the time. It hasn't caused any problems this summer, but we may have to do something before winter comes."

More than a half dozen broad stone steps led up to the front door of the library, and Roslyn moved up them quickly. The double doors, almost totally glass, were still locked, but after a quick knock, a small gray woman appeared from somewhere and looked questioningly at Roslyn, then pointed at the sign at one side of the door indicating the library's hours.

Roslyn waved at the woman and leaned close to the glass. Mouthing the words broadly, she said: "I'm the new librarian. Mrs. Sutherland said—"

Before she could say more, the woman smiled and nodded in understanding. She turned a lock and the door swung open.

"Come right in, Miss—Stratton, isn't it? Ruth told me about you." The door swung closed behind her, and the older woman turned the latch again. "Ruth—Mrs. Sutherland—isn't in yet, but she should be along any minute. I'm Mrs. Wellons, but call me Jenny."

"And I'm Roslyn, or Ros for short." She put out her hand, restraining her impulse to slouch in an effort to seem shorter, and took Mrs. Wellons' hand. Like the rest of the woman, it was thin, but there was a remarkable strength in it, Roslyn thought.

"All right, Ros. I suppose Ruth showed you around the place last week, didn't she?"

Roslyn nodded. "But she said I would be working mostly with the bookmobile, and I didn't get a chance to see that. It was out, she said."

Mrs. Wellons grinned. "Yes, I had it at one of the schools. I think it's really going to be quite popular with the kids out in the country schools. Why, you'd be surprised how many kids there are, even in this day and age, who have never even seen any books outside of the ones they have to use in school—and you know what most of the schoolbooks are like!"

"It's not just in the country schools, believe me," Roslyn said. "You should have heard some of the stories I heard in school. Some of the professors had worked in city libraries—big ones—and they said the same thing. There were—"

Roslyn stopped abruptly, laughing. "I'd better not get started on that. I have a dozen theories, probably all wrong, and a dozen solutions to the problems, probably all unworkable."

"That's all right, so do I. We'll have to compare notes sometime. But I think this bookmobile will help a lot—*if* we can keep Ruth from giving in to her natural tendency to be stuffy."

"Stuffy? In what way? She seemed nice enough last week."

Jenny shrugged her birdlike shoulders as she looked at Roslyn, who towered over the older woman by at least a half foot. "I shouldn't say stuffy, I suppose, not really. Conservative would be better. She's just a little careful when it comes to selecting books, especially for the schools. She's pretty good at it, usually, but last week she got a complaint from one of the teachers at a school we were at a couple of weeks before."

"Complaint? About what?"

"A book one of the kids in her class had gotten from the bookmobile. I don't even remember what the book was, but it was a mystery, a murder mystery, and a fairly good one at that. But this particular teacher has a hang-up about 'literary values,' and she didn't think we should carry that kind of 'trash' around to the schools. She feels the same way about science fiction—except maybe for things by Orwell, and I don't think she quite realizes that *1984* is science fiction. It's literature, so it can't be—" Jenny stopped, shrugging again. "See? I have my own soapbox, so I don't think you'll feel out of place around here."

"Apparently not," Roslyn said, laughing. "And you hit one of my favorite theories, too. Most of the people who complain about lack of literary value haven't ever read what they're complaining about. And you know—another theory of mine—I'm willing to bet that 'literary values' are one of the biggest reasons so many kids hate books by the time they get out of school. Too many teachers—and too many librarians, too, I'm afraid—insist that the kids read only what's 'good for them.'"

Mrs. Wellons nodded, smiling, and Roslyn found herself going on, warming to the subject. There was something about the small woman that invited Roslyn to open up. "The trouble is, to a kid in school, that kind of book is just plain dull. They're interested in other things. At least I know *I* was. So by the time they get out of school, they automatically think of books as something they had to read in school and nothing else. They never get the chance to find out there are a lot of books that are just plain fun."

Mrs. Wellons was nodding. "Just get them started is my motto," she said, "don't worry about what it is they get started on."

Roslyn couldn't help but laugh again. "You know, you sound just like Hubbard—he was one of the professors, a real revolutionary for someone his age. That's almost exactly what he said. Let them read horror stories or mysteries or adaptations of TV series or even comic books, just get them started reading before you lose them altogether. Once they realize there are things that are fun to read, they may even get into the habit. They might even decide they like it better than TV or comics. And someday, they might even find out they enjoy those things that were being stuffed down their throats before they were ready for them. You never know. If you don't—"

Roslyn stopped abruptly, noticing Mrs. Wellons' widening grin. "Sorry," Roslyn said, a little sheepishly, "but I warned you. And that's only the first couple of theories and solutions."

Still grinning, Jenny Wellons held her hand out to Roslyn. "Welcome to Fowler, Miss Stratton."

Roslyn took the hand and returned the grin. "Thank you, Mrs. Wellons," she said with a slight bow.

During the next half hour, before Mrs. Sutherland arrived a little after nine, Jenny Wellons gave Roslyn a quick tour through the paper mill. "Not that you'll ever be stuck with very much of this, of course, but it can't hurt to be prepared. The division between what library aides—like me—and librarians do isn't quite as strict as in your big city libraries. All of us have been known to do a little dusting and sweeping if the janitor doesn't make it in."

Before the tour was over, Roslyn had been introduced to a dozen or more forms and procedures, from checking out books to sending magazines out to the local bindery. She had even been introduced to Grommet, the library cat, a gray and white lump that spent most of its time on a sunny window ledge, either staring hungrily at birds outside or hopefully at library patrons inside. At the pace Jenny galloped through everything, Roslyn was lucky to remember a quarter of it, but at least, when it was over, she knew who to go to if she ever needed information on anything in the library—Jenny Wellons.

Mrs. Sutherland, a woman almost as tall as Roslyn, her graying hair pulled back in a tight bun this morning, gave Roslyn a key to the side door, located around the corner from the parking lot, and then took Roslyn out to look over the bookmobile. As they skimmed through the collection already on board, Roslyn, hoping she was being suitably subtle, got in a couple of comments about children's reading habits that she was sure Jenny would have appreciated.

"Do you think you can learn to drive this?" Mrs. Sutherland asked as they stood near the front door of the machine.

"Drive? You mean you don't have a driver?"

The older woman smiled. "Not unless we can find a volunteer. No, we feel lucky to have been able to afford a new librarian—you—let alone a driver. I'm afraid that, except for Jenny helping out occasionally, this will be a one-woman operation."

Roslyn shook her head. "I don't know. I've driven a car, of sorts, for three years, but I'm not sure about *this*."

"It shouldn't be too difficult. We knew that we would have to do the driving ourselves when we bought it, so we had it made as easy to operate as possible. An automatic shift, of course, and power steering."

"Of course." Roslyn eyed the bookmobile apprehensively as she and Mrs. Sutherland descended the steps to the ground, walked back to the library, and entered through the side door. Mrs. Sutherland stopped at her office, just to the left of the entrance, and Roslyn, responding to a "come-on-over" gesture from Jenny, walked over to the check-out desk, where Jenny was talking quietly to a young man, probably in his late twenties or early thirties. He was tall enough so that even Roslyn would have to look up at him, moderately handsome, and, she thought, remarkably well dressed for this early in the morning in a small town.

Or no, on second thought, make that very expensively dressed. She wasn't sure if it was the same thing. The shirt, a bright wine red, looked as if it were silk, and the trousers, a slightly darker shade of the same color, were so smooth and well-fitting that they reminded Roslyn of the models that were always shown in the ads for clothing stores. The jacket, a deep blue, was the same and, now that she thought about it, she realized that the face was, in a way, like the clothes. They went together. It wasn't movie-star handsome by any means, but it was certainly square-jawed enough so that no one would ever accuse him of having a weak chin. A few strands of near-black hair fell—were arranged? Roslyn wondered—semineatly over his forehead.

Jenny looked around as Roslyn walked up to join her behind the desk.

"Roslyn," she said, "meet your benefactor, if that's the word I want. In any event, this is Paul Blassingrame."

The man held out a hand across the check-out desk and Roslyn took it uncertainly.

"Very glad to meet you, Miss Stratton," he said, and his voice, though not particularly deep, was as smooth and well-fitting as his clothes. "I hope you enjoy our little town—and our little book-mobile."

"Thank you, Mr. Blassingrame. It's nice to meet you, too, but I don't quite understand—"

"It was the Blassingrame family," Jenny supplied, "that donated the money for the bookmobile. Particularly Paul, here."

"Oh? Well, I thank you very much, Mr. Blassingrame. Mrs. Wellons tells me it was really needed."

The man nodded, smiling. "Which, of course, is why I suggested the family provide the money." He shrugged. "But don't let the generosity of the gift overwhelm you. After all, it *is* tax deductible."

As they were talking, a middle-aged woman had approached the desk with a book, and Jenny moved over to check it out and chat briefly with her.

Paul Blassingrame leaned forward over the desk toward Roslyn. "I don't want to sound pushy about this, but have you had any experience driving anything as large as the bookmobile?"

Roslyn looked slightly startled at the question. "No, but according to Mrs. Sutherland it isn't very hard. I understand that Jenny— Mrs. Wellons—has been driving it until now."

He grinned, glancing sideways at the older woman, still chatting with the patron. "She has been, but—well, I don't want to discourage you, but what Jenny Wellons can do easily, many people can't do at all. If the truth were known, she runs more of the library than Mrs. Sutherland. Oh, not that Ruth isn't a capable person, but Jenny is the real spark plug around here."

Roslyn suppressed a laugh, not too successfully. "Yes, I've seen some of the sparks already."

Paul nodded, still grinning, and Roslyn couldn't help but think that, as grins went, it was reasonably attractive. Not overdone, but a hint of teeth. Semipro, like the hair, which was not really untidy, just slightly disarranged. Or perhaps she was being too suspicious, just because of his money and his clothes.

"And now," he said, "the reason I'm here—aside from simply meeting you, that is."

"Meeting me? How did you know—"

"Jenny told me, of course. Not long after you were hired last week, as a matter of fact. She keeps me well informed, especially in library matters." He chuckled softly. "In fact, she is as much responsible for the bookmobile as anyone. She can be very persuasive at times."

"I can imagine," Roslyn said, glancing toward Jenny, who had moved away from the desk to the card catalogue, where she was looking something up for a harried-looking teen-ager.

"But as I was saying," Paul continued, "my main reason for being here this morning is to offer my services as driving instructor. If you think you could use some instruction, that is."

"Considering that I've never driven anything larger than a Rambler, I'm sure I could use whatever help I can get. But are you sure that *you*—"

"That's settled, then." His voice left no doubt that the matter was, indeed, settled. He glanced around, located Jenny directing the teen-ager toward one of the shelves beyond the card catalogue.

"Jenny," Paul said as she returned to the desk, "tell Ruth that we'll be gone for a while. Driving lessons for the new recruit."

"Mr. Blassingame! I didn't say—" Roslyn began, a touch of annoyance in her voice, but she was cut off by Paul.

"You said you could use a lesson, didn't you? What better time than right now, before you get too bogged down in the daily routine? The weather is beautiful and the traffic is light. What more could you ask?"

"But Mrs. Sutherland may have other ideas," Roslyn persisted. "For one thing, before I do any bookmobiling or anything else, I have to take a little time to familiarize myself with the collection—find out what books we have and what we don't."

"It's all right," Jenny said, and Roslyn looked at her with

surprise. "In fact, if you want to do a little more than just have a driving lesson, you could go to one of the schools. We told the principal at Woodrow that we would try to get out there sometime this week; it's the only school we've missed so far this year. I was going to get it last week, but I had some kind of virus a couple of days last week. You go ahead. The bookmobile collection is filled up, so all you have to do is go."

Jenny glanced toward a clock on the wall to the left of the desk. "You can be there by ten," she went on. "That will be just about right. It usually takes a couple of hours to run everyone through, and by then it will be lunch time, and you can let a few of the real bookworms back in for a second look on their lunch hour. Yes, you go on ahead. I'll call Clifford—Mr. Baggerly, he's the principal—and let him know you're coming."

"But what about you?" Things were moving too fast, and Roslyn had an oddly helpless feeling that she didn't like, as if she were being simply swept along. "I thought you were going to be along, at least the first few times."

"Don't worry about it. It's not that different from here, except that the collection is smaller and the building is on wheels. You use the same check-out procedures. The only difference is that you use a stamp pad with red ink instead of black to stamp in the due dates. And the books will be due in—well, make it four weeks. Actually, they're due whenever the bookmobile gets around to the school again, and we don't have a real schedule made out yet. Just make it four weeks for now. Now get going. I'll tell Ruth where you are."

Jenny paused only long enough to get a set of ignition keys from a drawer and hand them to Roslyn before she bustled into Mrs. Sutherland's small office, leaving Roslyn and Paul Blassingrame standing across the desk from each other.

"What did I tell you?" Paul said. "Now do you begin to see why the library got the money for the bookmobile?"

Roslyn laughed. The helpless feeling was still there, but it wasn't as unpleasant as it had been at first. And, she realized, she would have to get used to it if she was going to have much to do with Jenny Wellons.

"I think I do," she said. "I'm only surprised that they didn't get it long ago."

"Not surprising. Jenny didn't meet me until last year—shortly

after she heard about the dialysis machine we'd given the hospital."
He moved around to the side of the desk and held out his hand.
"Now, are you ready? Or are you waiting for Ruth's official, if auto-
matic, blessing?"

Roslyn glanced toward the office. The door was open and Mrs.
Sutherland was nodding as Jenny talked. They both glanced toward the desk, and the head librarian nodded, smiling. Jenny
picked up the phone on Mrs. Sutherland's desk and began dialing
at the same time she made a "get moving" motion with the receiver
to Roslyn and Paul.

With a final chuckle, Roslyn grabbed her purse from under the
check-out desk and the two of them made their way to the bookmobile. Grommet, Roslyn noticed, was in the window facing the
parking area, and his eyes followed them intently, as if he thought
they were a pair of giant birds. She wondered briefly how he would
like a ride in the bookmobile, but quickly decided that he would be
more of a distraction than he was worth at the schools. And a bookmobile full of unknown kids is not the safest place for a cat.

"We'd better have the lesson on the way back," Roslyn said, as
they climbed into the machine, "if we're going to be at that school
by ten. You do know where—what was that name again?"

"Woodrow," he said, sliding into the driver's seat. "Yes, I know
where it is. It's only five or six miles out, on old Highway 31."

Roslyn seated herself behind the desk and began a quick inven-
tory as Paul started the engine and pulled away from the curb. The
small file box for cards of checked-out books, already containing a
half dozen subdivisions: Burton, Reiter, Richland Center, Athens,
Woodrow, and Macy. All but Woodrow had two or three dozen
cards already. The red ink pad. The stamps, and the box of rubber
letters and numbers to make the due dates with. A file drawer built
into the desk, apparently meant to be a card catalogue but still
empty.

Paul pulled easily into traffic on Main Street and headed south,
past the Heyde's sign.

"Now," he said over his shoulder, "if you're going to be my student for the day, suppose you tell me something about yourself. Are
you from Fowler originally?"

Roslyn looked up from the due-date stamp she was assembling.
"Only slightly," she said. "I've lived most of my life in Wisconsin."

"And you got your Master's in library science from the University of Wisconsin this summer. How did you happen to end up down here?"

She was silent for a moment as she finished with the stamp and returned the box of type to the drawer. "I see Jenny must have filled you in pretty well. But if you already know all about me, why ask?"

He laughed disarmingly. "I know that you went to school in Wisconsin and lived there for at least as long as you went to school. But that's about all. And I'm curious as to why and how someone from that far away ever found her way to Barton County. I have to admit that Fowler is not my idea of the 'Good Life.'" As he spoke, she could hear the capital letters in his tone.

"You and my cousin," she said. "Vivian seems to find it hard to believe, too."

"Your cousin? Then you at least have relatives here?"

"My mother's brother and his daughter. Carl and Vivian Jefferson. I'm staying with them until I find myself an apartment. Or a house. As for myself, I *am* originally from Fowler, in a manner of speaking."

"Yes? I thought one was either from a place or one was not." He glanced back at her as they stopped at a traffic light at the south end of Fowler. Highway 31 slanted off to the left while 25 went straight ahead. He touched the left-turn signal and set it blinking.

"My parents left Fowler when I was less than a year old," Roslyn said. "I can't say that I remember much about the town."

"Your parents . . ." He frowned thoughtfully as he made the left jog onto 31. "The Strattons, I presume?"

"Thomas and Alicia Stratton, yes."

He shook his head slightly. "I can't quite place the names. But, then, names have never been my strong point. Are they people I *should* remember? For any reason other than the fact that they produced a lovely daughter?"

She looked up, trying to see his face in the rearview mirror, but she couldn't. Unable to see the expression on his face, she decided it was safest to ignore the remark altogether. By stretching the imagination a bit, she might be called statuesque, or, by stretching it even further, striking, although her own opinion in recent years had leaned toward things like "big-boned." Her college roommate, trying to be complimentary, had once likened her to a "tall Joan Crawford," and she supposed the comparison was fair, if remote.

Even so, she had never considered Joan Crawford to be one of the great beauties of the world. No, "lovely" was stretching things a bit far, particularly compared to the kind of women that someone as rich and—studiedly?—handsome as Paul Blassingrame was undoubtedly accustomed to.

"Dad owned a small print shop," she said noncommittally. "Nothing on the level of the Blassingrame holdings, I'm sure."

"A print shop? Not the one on Eighth Street? Across from the courthouse?"

"I have no idea. As I said, I remember practically nothing from the first year of my life."

He laughed. "Nor do I. But the next time you talk to your father, find out. If that's the one, it did end up being part of the 'Blassingrame holdings,' as you put it."

For a moment, the rainy gloom of the night before reached out for Roslyn, but she pushed it back quickly and smiled as she answered. "I'll ask my mother. It might be a bit hard to ask Dad, unless you know a good medium."

Paul Blassingrame was silent for a hundred yards or more. "Sorry," he said finally, quietly. "I didn't know."

"That's all right. No reason you should have. Besides, it's been several years. It's practically ancient history now." Not quite, a voice inside her said. There's something about a life being ended that abruptly, that unexpectedly, that lingers on. If nothing else, it makes you realize—too late—that there are a lot of things you never found out about that person, a lot of things that you really wanted to find out and talk about but never quite got around to. After all, you thought, there was still plenty of time. And it makes you wonder about other people. It makes you want to get closer, to find out what there is inside them that never shows up on the surface, things that would make you know and understand them better.

Involuntarily, Roslyn found herself once again wondering about her mother's reaction to Roslyn's decision to move to Fowler. It had seemed so unlike her in one way, to try to discourage Roslyn from doing what she wanted to do. She had never done anything like that before, not that Roslyn could remember. Yet, when Roslyn remembered the way that her mother—and her father—had always avoided all mention of Fowler, perhaps it was not so different . . .

Roslyn blinked, realizing that Paul was speaking to her again.

"What was that?" she asked. "I'm afraid my mind was wandering."

"I was just trying to make amends. I was asking if you have anything planned for next Saturday evening."

"Not unless I'm still apartment hunting," she said, and her mind came fully back to the present. "Or unless I've already found one and I've managed to talk my mother into coming to visit me, which is pretty unlikely."

"Which is unlikely? Finding an apartment or getting your mother to visit?"

"Getting her to visit me. The way she's been acting since I told her about this job, you'd think Fowler was the Black Hole of Calcutta."

Paul shrugged. "Well, as I said before, each to his or her own. It's not exactly my first choice among the great pleasure spots of the world, but it's where the money—Blassingrame money, at least—is located. But that's neither here nor there, to coin a phrase. What about Saturday night? You can't spend all your time house hunting. And if your mother surprises you and shows up, bring her along."

"Bring her along? To what?"

"Next Saturday, the annual Blassingrame Birthday Blast is being held. Sophie, the oldest surviving Blassingrame, will be— Well, she'll be eighty-something, sometime this week or next. The exact age and date are academic, but the annual gathering of the clan, plus a few dozen non-Blassingrames, will be held Saturday. And I would be honored if you would consent to be one of the non-Blassingrames in attendance. And your mother, too, if she's here."

"Are there a lot of Blassingrames?"

"More than enough to go around, I'm sure. They don't all live around Fowler, of course, but they still manage to drag themselves back to see Sophie once each year. Or to be seen *by* Sophie, I should say. The will, you know. Sophie still controls most everything worth being controlled. Oh, she delegates some authority, mostly to my father, but she keeps the strings pretty tight. All of which is just another added attraction to an objective observer such as yourself. You probably won't get many opportunities to see the effects of so many strings on so many people. Really quite fascinating."

He raised his eyes to look in the rearview mirror. "Well, how about it? Will you come?"

"You make it sound like quite a zoo."

"Just wait till you see it in person. Well?"

"Why not? But tell me, if I come, can I bring someone with me?"

"Of course," he said quickly, then paused. "On the other hand, maybe. Who did you have in mind?"

"My cousin, Vivian."

He shrugged. "Certainly. Your uncle, too, if you want."

"Thanks, but—" She stopped abruptly, cutting the words off.

"What's the matter?" Paul asked as Roslyn lapsed into silence. "Do I detect a note of hostility between you and your uncle?"

She shook her head. "I hardly know him. I met him for the first time last night. It's just that—" She stopped, restraining her normal impulse to explain the whole odd relationship between Vivian and her father.

"Yes?" Paul prompted.

"Nothing," she said. "We just got off on the wrong foot, that's all."

He shrugged. "None of my business, in any event. I've already put my foot in my mouth once too often this morning. You're welcome with whomever you wish to bring—cousin, uncle, mother, or any combination thereof. All right?"

She looked up at the rearview mirror again and saw his eyes watching her speculatively. His eyes . . .

She blinked and looked away. For an instant, just a brief instant, there had been something there—something familiar, something that, somewhere, sometime, she had seen before . . .

But what? She looked up again, but Paul had returned his full attention to the road and she couldn't see him in the mirror. For several seconds she watched the mirror, but he did not look up. Finally, she shook her head as if to clear it and resolutely returned her attention to her desk and the file of checked-out books.

CHAPTER 3

The gift shop, just beyond the city limits on a fair-sized, wooded lot with a gravel parking area next to the building, had at one time been the front room of the house. A large bay window had been converted into a display window, and a sign—HANNEMAN'S GIFTS—had been projected out from above the window. While much of the display was given over to the usual mass-produced knickknacks, it also contained a remarkable array of obviously homemade dolls, ranging from tiny things made from pipe cleaners and acorns to huge, multicolored clowns made from whole skeins of yarn.

The orange and purple and yellow clowns were what had first caught Roslyn's eye as she and Paul Blassingrame had driven past on their way back from Woodrow two days before, but it was a smaller, almost colorless doll in one corner of the window that had brought her back for a second, closer look. At the time, from the vantage point of the moving bookmobile, she had gotten only a glimpse, and she had been sure that the doll could not possibly be what it appeared to be.

Now, standing with her face only inches from the display window glass, she saw that her first impression had been correct. The doll, obviously a one-of-a-kind creation and not something that had been stamped out of a plastic mold, was about a foot high. Its head and hands were made of a rough, grayish material that reminded Roslyn of unfinished concrete, and its entire body, including arms and legs, was wrapped in frayed and soiled strips of once-white cloth. Its right arm was crooked tightly against its chest, and its legs were positioned to give the impression of slow, shambling motion. It was, as she had first suspected, the limping, bedraggled, put-upon mummy that had spread terror (and unintentional laughter) through a half dozen movies back in the forties and a thousand "Late-Late Shows" in the sixties and seventies. Roslyn herself had come across Kharis—and Larry Talbot and Igor and the Monster and the Creature and a hundred other leftover horrors—for the first time rather late in life for that sort of thing. Her freshman roommate at college had been an addict already, and Roslyn had soon become one. She never knew quite what it was that appealed to her about them. They weren't, for the most part, particularly terrifying, nor even nostalgic, but somehow, once one appeared on the screen late at night, she found herself looking up from her books more and more often until, finally, she was staring at it with the same fascination and making the same sort of comments as her roommate.

Maybe, she often thought, it was simply an elaborate disguise for procrastination that her subconscious had worked out. Or maybe it was because, in a weird sort of way, she identified with them, big and gawky and vaguely out of place, but she didn't like to think of that too often. She had thought of it more than enough when, at twelve, she had realized she was taller than her mother, and again at fourteen when she had grown past her father's five feet seven. After a time, though, she had given up trying to analyze her addiction or cure herself of it. If there was something she absolutely had to get done on monster nights, she would settle in at the university library a half dozen blocks away and return to her room only after either the movies were over or her work was done.

Not far from the miniature Kharis in the window was a smaller doll, this one dressed completely in black and bearing a vague resemblance to Larry Talbot on the night of the full moon. It, too, had to be unique, she thought. The head, once Roslyn bent down to peer at it more closely, seemed to be made of a gigantic, hairy seed of some kind.

A bell over the shop door tinkled and Roslyn glanced up. A small, wiry woman, probably in her fifties, stood on the small porch just outside the door.

"It's a mango seed," the woman said, indicating the Wolfman's head. "It started out to be a farmer when I first made it, but Trina —one of the girls that helps out in the summer, during the tourist season—thought it looked more like a werewolf."

"She was right," Roslyn said, laughing. "Is that your monster collection in this corner?"

The older woman's smile broadened. "It didn't start out to be, but that's how it turned out. It's mostly Trina's doing, though. She started watching all those movies on TV last summer, and since then everything reminds her of a vampire or a werewolf."

"Or a mummy," Roslyn added. "What's that one made of?"

"Papier-mâché. Usually mâché is much smoother than that, like George Washington up there in the other corner. You sand it down after you put the features in and it's dried out, but Trina saw this one before I had a chance to do any sanding. She was so insistent that it looked like a mummy that she made the body and dressed it —or wrapped it—herself."

"You make all your own dolls, then?" Roslyn asked.

The woman nodded. "Everything else, though, except for a little jewelry and small ceramics, is strictly commercial—all the mottos and glass animals and paperweights and novelties."

"You certainly have a variety of dolls."

"This is nothing. Come inside and look around."

"Thank you, but I—"

"Don't worry, I'm not about to start a sales pitch. Think of it as a museum. I like an audience as well as a customer any day."

Roslyn glanced at her watch, saw that she still had a half hour to go on her lunch hour. "All right," she said, and followed the older woman into the shop.

Inside were several counters of the usual gift shop items—ash trays with slogans, aprons with slogans, drinking glasses with slogans, and so on—but one entire wall was taken up with long shelves of dolls. As in the window, they were all shapes and sizes. An octopus made of green yarn. A Kaiser Wilhelm with a long-nosed gourd for a head and a piece of black felt for a walrus mustache. An Andy Capp made of black pipe cleaners and an unusually flat-topped acorn. A cowboy with a round cork for a head and a wishbone giving it permanently bowed legs. An Uncle Sam with—?

"Soap," the older woman said. "Carved soap. The beard is cotton from an aspirin bottle."

Roslyn laughed. "And those?" She lifted her arm and pointed at the top row. "They're so lifelike . . ."

The dollmaker's eyes followed the direction of the finger to the shelf, but then momentarily returned to Roslyn's hand, and then to her face. For an instant, the woman's forehead creased in the suggestion of a troubled frown.

"They're wax," she said, her eyes returning to the dolls. "A few of them were made by my mother before she died. They're the expensive ones, which is why they're on the top shelf, out of reach of small children and dogs. They take a lot of time and they sell mostly to collectors, not to your casual tourist. Like these others—" She pointed to a glass case further along the wall. A half dozen dolls, paler and less lifelike, looking almost like miniature death masks, rested behind the glass.

"Those are bisque," the woman said, "that's fired clay. For a time, back around the turn of the century, our family was fairly well known among doll collectors, but . . ." She shrugged lightly. "The last few years, though, I have, as the big companies would say, 'diversified.' For one thing, I don't have quite the knack for it that my ancestors did. For another, it's more fun this way, even if I don't make as much money."

The dollmaker glanced down for a moment, then back at Roslyn's face. "By the way, my name is Frieda Hanneman." She held out her hand.

"Roslyn Stratton," Roslyn said, taking the hand lightly.

"Are you just passing through?" Frieda Hanneman's eyes met Roslyn's directly, and her hand still held Roslyn's.

Roslyn shook her head. "No, I'll be living in Fowler—or somewhere nearby. I just started work at the library this week."

"I see." Still the woman did not release Roslyn's hand. She looked down at it now, and Roslyn could not help but notice a slight nervousness in the gesture.

"Yes," Roslyn went on, some of the woman's nervousness transferring itself to her, "I'm staying with my cousin now, but I'm looking for an apartment. You wouldn't know of any, would you? The only ones I've seen advertised in the paper haven't been quite what I'm after."

Frieda Hanneman's eyes came up again to meet Roslyn's before she spoke. "No, I don't, but I'll keep an eye out for you." Again she hesitated, as if she were about to continue, and she looked around the room once again.

"Do you have a workshop?" Roslyn asked, more to fill the silence than anything else. "Where you make the dolls?"

The woman nodded, as if relieved that Roslyn had continued the conversation. "Yes, it's right through that door." She pointed to a half-open door behind one of the counters. "Would you like to see it?"

Roslyn started to shake her head, but then thought for a moment. In addition to taking care of the bookmobile, she was supposed to be thinking of possible programs the library could present to the local children. Nothing would probably come of it until next summer, during the summer vacation, but it wouldn't hurt to have something in mind. Something like, she thought, having someone come in and demonstrate dollmaking . . .

"Yes," she said, "if it wouldn't be too much trouble."

"Of course not." The woman was smiling again, some of the tension gone. "As I said, I like an audience as well as a customer any day. I'm afraid I don't have the true professional spirit." She led the way back around the counter.

"Have you ever demonstrated your dollmaking?" Roslyn asked. "To any of the schools? Or local groups?"

"I go to the high school once or twice each year," she said, pushing open the door to the back room and motioning Roslyn through. "The winters are always a little slow here at the shop."

As Roslyn stepped into the room, Mrs. Hanneman flipped a switch, and a pair of long fluorescent tubes in the center of the ceiling flickered into life, supplementing the sunlight that glared in through the single large window on the right. A large, sturdy-looking table—a workbench, really—took up most of the center of the room under the lights. The walls, except for a battered couch near the window, were lined with shelves and metal cabinets and glass-fronted cabinets and pegboards. Jugs and jars and cans and tools filled most of the shelves, and one of the glass-fronted cabinets was full of spare parts—heads, arms, legs, torsos, everything. Dozens of tiny wigs hung on long pegs stuck out from one of the pegboards. An electric sewing machine was set up on one corner of the work table, and a box overflowing with hundreds of scraps of cloth lay nearby. A cubic metal box, looking vaguely like a small safe, sat on a metal stand at the back edge of the table.

"I don't use half of this stuff more than once every five years," Mrs. Hanneman said, gesturing at the cluttered shelves and cabinets, "but just as sure as I'd get rid of something, I'd find a perfect use for it about two days later."

"I know what you mean," Roslyn agreed, looking around at the huge assortment of odds and ends. "I recognize a lot of the things, but that, there—" She pointed at the heavy-looking metal box on its stand on the table.

"A kiln," Mrs. Hanneman said, "just a small one. It's for firing ceramics, like those bisque dolls. I don't use it very often. In fact, about all I do with it nowadays is take it to the high school for my demonstrations. Mother used to have a larger one that she kept in the basement."

For the next ten minutes, until Roslyn glanced at her watch and saw that she would have to hurry to get back to the library before her lunch hour was over, Mrs. Hanneman moved about the room, keeping up a running commentary on everything from the kiln ("four or five times as hot as a regular oven") to the dozen or so carved apples and pears she had hanging in one corner ("The sort of thing anyone can do. No matter what the carving looks like at the start, by the time they're dried, they're all monsters of one kind or another.").

As they moved back into the shop and Roslyn started toward the front door, Mrs. Hanneman spoke again, and Roslyn could hear the tension return to her voice with each syllable.

"Miss Stratton, I—I couldn't help but notice your ring."

Roslyn stopped and half turned back toward the woman. She glanced down at the ring, and a faint tremor ran through her for no logical reason. "Yes, it is a bit unusual."

"Yes, it's most unusual," Mrs. Hanneman said slowly. "It—looks almost like an eye. I can't remember ever seeing an opal—it *is* an opal, isn't it?—cut like that."

Roslyn nodded, looking at it again. She had never thought of it as looking like an eye, but now that Mrs. Hanneman mentioned it . . . a faint tingling seemed to move about, somewhere deep inside her.

"Yes," Roslyn said finally, "an Australian fire opal, or so I've been told. I've often wondered about the odd shape. No jeweler has ever had the slightest idea why it would have been cut that way. It *is* pretty, though, even if it isn't your standard opal."

"Yes, very beautiful." The woman hesitated again, looking up into Roslyn's face, as if searching for something. She was a totally different woman from the open, cheerful woman who had been happily chattering away in the workroom a minute before. "If you don't mind my asking, where did you get it?"

Roslyn laughed, again picking up some of the nervousness from the other woman. "I don't mind, but I'm afraid I don't have an answer."

"I'm sorry. I didn't mean to—"

"No, it's perfectly all right. It's just that I don't know where it came from. I've had it all—well, *almost* all my life. My mother tells me I found it, although I certainly don't remember anything about it. I've had the opal itself ever since I can remember, a sort of good-luck piece. I had it made into a ring when I started high school. Or rather, my mother did, as a gift. She was always—" Roslyn stopped, shaking her head. As always when she got the least bit nervous, she was talking a blue streak.

"You said it was a good-luck piece," Mrs. Hanneman said then. "I hope I'm not being too nosy, but . . . ?"

And you're encouraging me to babble on, Roslyn thought. "No, not at all," she said, "but I'm afraid I can't be of much help. I don't know where it came from. I was so small at the time, not even a year old, that I don't remember finding it at all. It was here in Fowler someplace, just before we moved away, but that's about all I know."

Frieda Hanneman's eyes snapped up to Roslyn's face, as if searching it with a new intensity. She swallowed audibly, and then: "Your mother? Does *she* know where you found it?"

Roslyn shook her head. "I don't think so," she said, and then, inevitably, hurried on: "It's always been a family mystery. I'm told that my mother found it clutched in my hand one day, and I wouldn't let it go. I screamed my head off whenever she tried to take it away from me. She had to wait until I was asleep to get it out of my hand. At least, that's the story I've heard."

"But you have no idea where it might have come from originally?"

"None. It's a complete mystery. Or so my mother tells me."

"But you said it was a—a good-luck piece. Didn't you?"

Roslyn shrugged. "My mother always called it that. I'm told I found it—or it found me—about the time I had the flu. Or just after. I guess she considered it a piece of luck that I survived at all. I understand there were a few that didn't."

The dollmaker nodded, and her eyes seemed to retreat. For a moment there was a glaze to them, as if they had come unfocused. "Flu," she said, her voice as distant as her eyes. "A new strain of flu virus."

"That's right," Roslyn said, nodding. "Children were especially vulnerable, apparently. Or so Mother said. I guess I *was* lucky. I sometimes think my close call had something to do with my parents moving away from here."

Frieda Hanneman nodded, her eyes gradually returning to the present. "Yes, there were deaths. Not many, but enough. More than enough."

And Roslyn suddenly thought: Mrs. Hanneman lost someone in that epidemic. That's why she's so interested. That was why she got so misty-eyed when I mentioned it.

But now, as Roslyn looked at the woman again, the lined face was completely composed, a look of polite interest on it, and Roslyn wondered at the sudden change.

"Your parents," Mrs. Hanneman said speculatively, "I wonder if I knew them. You said they moved away. Just when was that?"

"I'm not sure of the exact date. About twenty years ago—twenty-one, actually. I'm twenty-two now, and I was less than a year old when we moved."

Another interested nod. "Mr. and Mrs. Stratton? I don't seem to remember the name, I'm afraid. But, then, my memory has never been exceptional."

"You might have known my father. He owned a print shop, although I don't know where it was located. He never talked much about it."

"A print shop?" Though the voice remained steady, a faint note of tension seemed to enter it once again. "I seem to remember a print shop, somewhere in the middle of town. It *was* in Fowler, wasn't it? Not in one of the other towns in the county?"

"As far as I know. At least no other town was ever mentioned." Roslyn forced a short laugh. "But, then, Fowler was rarely mentioned, either."

The older woman seemed to take in the information carefully. "As I said," she resumed after a moment, "I seem to remember a print shop up on Eighth Street, right across from the courthouse. It's where the Fowler *Journal* offices are located now."

"It's possible. I suppose I really should look into it, now that I'm here." Another laugh, still partly forced. "After all, Fowler has been pretty much of a mystery town to me all these years."

Mrs. Hanneman smiled disarmingly, but her eyes remained intently on Roslyn. "My family has lived here for generations," she said, "and it often appears to be a mystery to me, too. But tell me, where have you been living since you left?"

"Wisconsin. A small town not far from Milwaukee. My father bought another print shop there."

A brief hesitation, and then the woman said: "I have some relatives in Wisconsin. What town was it?"

"Hartland. Nobody has ever heard of it."

Mrs. Hanneman shook her head. "My niece lives around Madison."

"I went to school there for five years—until a couple of months ago, in fact."

"A lovely town. I've visited it a number of times. Not as often as I'd like, but . . . no, I'm afraid I don't know Hartland. Does your father still own the print shop there?"

Roslyn shook her head. "He died several years ago."

"I'm sorry. I didn't—"

"That's all right. I was in high school at the time. It was several years ago."

"And your mother . . . ?"

"She still lives in Hartland. I've been trying to get her to come to visit me here, but I'm not having much luck."

"Yes, that would be nice. You shouldn't lose touch with your family." Again there was a distant quality to the older woman's voice, and once again Roslyn thought: Yes, she lost someone, and it still bothers her. Inwardly, a little bitterly, Roslyn laughed. Unlike me, she thought. Such things don't affect me at all.

Then, before either of them could say more, they were startled by the sound of the shop door opening and the bell tinkling loudly. With those everyday sounds, the outside world—the sunlight baking in through the display window, the sound of a truck laboring by on the highway—came sharply into focus again. Roslyn glanced hurriedly at her watch again. She would certainly be late getting back now . . .

With a final nod to the dollmaker, Roslyn turned and hurried past the new customer, who stood fingering one of the motto-covered aprons displayed near the door. Roslyn pushed quickly through the door and hurried down the steps and around to her car, parked at the corner of the building. The sun was hot, too hot for late September, and the air was almost totally still. As she pulled out onto the highway, she glanced back once. Frieda Hanneman, silent and expressionless, was visible through the door, her eyes following Roslyn as if the customer standing next to her didn't exist.

Roslyn shivered despite the heat and, with an effort, returned her eyes to the highway. Though she knew it was her imagination, she could feel the dollmaker's eyes on her back as she accelerated rapidly down the highway, pushing the Rambler just a little harder than she really should have.

CHAPTER 4

"The Blassingrames!" Vivian said for at least the fifth time during the five-mile drive. "I still can't really believe we're going!"

She looked nervously once again at the rust-red skirt and pale sweater she was wearing, contrasting them with the utilitarian dark blue pantsuit that Roslyn wore. "You're *sure* it isn't formal? I always thought—"

"Relax, Viv, relax!" Roslyn said, wishing she could take her own advice a little more. Compared to her cousin, she was relatively calm, but it was very definitely only relatively. It was better now than it had been ten minutes before, when they had left the house, but it was still not perfect by any means. She still felt the traces of nervous perspiration under her arms, and she was glad that, after all the debating with herself, she had decided that her burnt-orange outfit was a bit too spectacular for a large group of mostly strangers and had settled on the much less spectacular dark blue one. Not only would the dark blue show stains less, but it would, she told herself, attract less attention, which would, in turn, give her less reason to be nervous. Vivian's open nervousness, though, an exaggeration of Roslyn's own internal tension, seemed to be having a calming effect on her. Or maybe it was her own lectures to Vivian, telling her to calm down, that were doing it. Maybe she was really starting to believe them, emotionally as well as intellectually.

"Relax," she said again, "it's just a birthday party. You've been to birthday parties before, haven't you?"

"Yes, but not *Blassingrame* birthday parties!"

"Don't worry about it," Roslyn said, and she could feel another notch of her own tension slipping away even as she spoke. "They're just people, like everyone else. Paul, in fact, is quite nice, even if he is something of a playboy. He's driven the bookmobile for me twice this week. If it helps you any, just think of him as a wealthy book-mobile driver."

Vivian laughed, as much from nervousness as from amusement, and leaned back into the seat stiffly. "That's all right for *you* to say. You know him. And you've had—"

"Vivian!" Roslyn cut her off sharply. "If you tell me one more time how worldly I am compared to you, I swear I'll—I'll turn around and drive back home and we'll spend the rest of the evening watching reruns!"

Vivian lowered her eyes and was silent, and Roslyn glanced toward her again. At the expression on her cousin's face, Roslyn had to laugh, and with the laugh even more of the remaining tension slid away. For the first time in the last hour, she was close to being relaxed.

"I'm sorry, Viv," she said, her voice its normal, quiet self once again. "Just take it easy and take the evening a piece at a time. Everything will work out fine."

Vivian said nothing, but Roslyn thought that, beneath the tension, she could detect a faint, anticipatory smile.

Ahead, in the lingering dusk, a pair of lights appeared, topping the stone pillars that marked the entrance to the Blassingrame estate, and a minute later they were turning between the pillars and moving up the long, curving drive. The house, invisible behind the trees at first, appeared suddenly as they rounded a final curve.

Roslyn frowned. For just an instant, the scene seemed to shift before her eyes, and a faint tingling spread over her like a fleeting electrical charge.

Apprehension? *Déjà vu?* Or . . . ?

It was, she realized, the same kind of feeling that had struck her when she had glimpsed Paul's eyes in the mirror in the bookmobile. A feeling of—familiarity? But she had never seen the Blassingrame house before, so it could hardly be that. Unless there had been a picture, in a newspaper, or a book . . .

The house was, Roslyn had to admit, impressive enough to have been photographed for publication, and she wondered who the architect had been. It was two full stories high with a series of pointed towers jutting sharply into the fading sky above them. In the semidarkness, the material looked gray and stony, but she couldn't be sure. Whatever it was, it would have looked perfectly at home behind a moat and drawbridge.

The drive made a large loop past the front of the house—mansion —and Roslyn pulled to a stop at the end of a line of twenty or thirty cars. Compared to most of the vehicles, her Rambler looked like a very poor branch of the family indeed. Aside from a VW and a couple of recent compacts and subcompacts, nothing looked as if it would have sold for less than a full year of Roslyn's salary, before taxes. One looked suspiciously as if it were made for a chauffeur.

A uniformed butler opened the front door for them, but before anything could be said or Roslyn's recently dissipated nervousness could rebuild itself, Paul Blassingrame appeared and motioned the butler away with a wave of his hand.

"Roslyn! Happy as hell you could make it. Maybe the evening won't be a total loss after all." He gave her a quick peck on the cheek before turning to Vivian, who was standing by, wide-eyed.

"And this, of course, is Cousin Vivian." He reached down from his lofty height of six-three or six-four and, before Vivian could react, brushed his lips lightly across her forehead. "Short Cousin Vivian. Very glad to make your acquaintance." He held out his hand.

Vivian, still flustered, took the hand for an instant, then dropped it. "Very nice to meet you, Mr.—" She hesitated uncertainly, looking toward Roslyn.

"I'm sorry," Roslyn said, laughing. "This is Paul Blassingrame. The wealthy bookmobile driver I told you about."

"I had hoped to be on to bigger and better things by now," he said, "but your cousin is determined not to become proficient in bookmobile driving. It may take another half dozen lessons, or even more."

"One or two will do it, I'm sure," Roslyn put in. "You are, however, more than welcome to continue your present volunteer library service as long as you wish. I understand that in more civilized areas of the world there are bookmobiles with a permanent staff of two—or even three, including a driver."

He shrugged eloquently and took Roslyn's hand in one of his own and Vivian's in the other. "But Fowler, of course, is not all that civilized. Present company excepted, of course."

He led them down the broad, high-ceilinged hall and through a mammoth arching door. The room beyond was filled with people and voices. The only ones in formal dress seemed to be two butlers and three or four maids who were continually circulating and moving, doing whatever it was that butlers and maids did at such gatherings.

Once inside the room, Paul released his grip on their hands.

"Sophie has not made her grand entrance yet," he said, "so there is still time to mingle. If there are indeed any amongst us with whom you have a desire to mingle. And of course there are always" —he motioned with his right hand, a casual gesture, and a maid carrying a tray of drinks materialized from somewhere—"fortifications," he concluded, taking a small glass of amber liquid from the tray.

Roslyn searched through the drinks and settled on what appeared to be a bacardi. A small sip proved her right, but it also proved that it was stronger than she was used to. Not that, she thought, she had ever had the chance to get really used to even weak ones. Cocktail parties are few and far between for largely self-supporting college students.

Vivian shook her head, smiling nervously. "Nothing for me, thank you."

"Your own choice, of course," Paul said, and the maid vanished as quickly as she had appeared. "In case you regret your decision, it is always easily reversed—as I strongly suspect it will be before much mingling has been accomplished. And now—"

He finished off his own drink in a single gulp, set the empty glass on a nearby table, and held his hands up in an impresario gesture. "Are you ready? All right, then, Miss Stratton, Miss Jefferson, on the count of three. One. Two." He looked from Roslyn to Vivian and back. "Ready? Three! Mingle!"

He brought his arms down and swept his hands outward, palms out in the manner of someone making a grand presentation. He stood like that for a second, and then, when Roslyn only laughed, he shrugged elaborately.

"Very well," he began again, "you have had your chance and you have—you will pardon the cliché—blown it. Henceforth you shall both be subject to—" His eyes swept around the room, then back to the two women. "You shall both be subject to—enforced mingling! On a limited scale at first, of course. A Blassingrame Blast is not the ideal environment for a novice mingler to undertake full-scale operations without a preliminary warm-up period."

Again he looked around the room. No one seemed to be paying him the slightest attention. After a moment he apparently spotted someone he had been looking for, and he shepherded the women halfway across the room, expertly guiding them through and past the clumps of people. At the foot of a broad, curving staircase, like something out of an old movie, he stopped.

An older man, perhaps in his fifties, dressed in conservative gray slacks and dark sports jacket, stood near the bottom of the stairs, looking toward the hallway that was just visible at the top. He was at least as tall as Paul, considerably over six feet, and, despite the graying crew cut and the deeply etched lines in his face, Roslyn could see a strong resemblance to Paul.

"Awaiting the queen?" At Paul's voice, the older man turned abruptly. A scowl darkened his face for an instant, but then the craggy features softened as his eyes fell on Vivian and Roslyn.

"Ladies," Paul went on, "may I present the aging heir apparent, my father. Benjamin Blassingrame by name. Father, I'd like you to meet Roslyn Stratton and Vivian Jefferson."

At Paul's first words, the scowl had returned momentarily and the older man's eyes had darted toward Paul, but as he reached out and took their hands one at a time, the smile returned.

"Very pleased to meet you, Miss Stratton, Miss Jefferson. You will have to excuse my son if he seems a bit—"

"Not true," Paul broke in. "You do not have to excuse me at all." He shrugged. "Although, of course, it is standard procedure for you to do so. And it *would* be rather nice if you did. I am, after all, your favorite bookmobile driver."

He turned back to his father. "Miss Stratton is the new librarian in Fowler. She will be operating the Blassingrame Bookmobile."

The frown returned to the older man's face. "Paul!"

Paul grinned loosely. "If I may be allowed to return the favor, you will have to forgive my father, Misses Stratton and Jefferson. He is of the old school, which believes that one's charities should be kept to oneself—except for the Internal Revenue Service, of course, who are always among the very first to know."

He held up his hand, as if to forestall another sharp word from his father. "And now," Paul went on, "shall we begin again? Miss Roslyn Stratton, Miss Vivian Jefferson, this is my father, Benjamin Blassingrame."

This time the introductions went more conventionally, and, after a minute or two of explaining how Roslyn liked Fowler and how much Vivian appreciated the invitation to the party, they were ushered away by Paul and introduced, as promised, to a number of

Blassingrames, pseudo-Blassingrames, and non-Blassingrames. After a half hour and at least two dozen new faces and names, Vivian finally relented and accepted what Paul insisted was a very mild cocktail.

Not long after, Paul introduced them to "Tom Lory, our resident dwarf on the City Council, not only the shortest but also the youngest. And one of the more ambitious."

Roslyn flushed slightly at the reference to height but managed to keep from slouching as she shook hands with Lory. Actually, he was only a couple of inches shorter than Roslyn, at least five and a half feet, but compared to the Blassingrame men, all of whom seemed to top six feet, he did tend to stand out in the crowd.

The comparative shortness of Lory and Vivian—as well as, perhaps, the cocktail—seemed to provide a good starting point for them, and, after a minute, almost unnoticed by Vivian, Roslyn eased away from them, taking Paul with her. Paul, watching the maneuver with exaggerated intensity, grinned but said nothing until they were at least two or three conversations removed from Vivian and Lory and in no danger of being overheard.

"I suspect," Paul said, as Roslyn came to a stop and glanced back toward the couple, "that there is a touch of Jenny Wellons in you."

"Jenny? What is that supposed to mean?"

He laughed. "As if you didn't know what Jenny was up to! How do you think that I knew a beautiful"—he hesitated, leaning back and wrinkling his brow in concentrated observation for a moment—"that a rather attractive young lady was starting at the library last Monday morning? All right? And don't try to tell me that you brought Cousin Vivian to this party simply to keep you company."

Roslyn started to protest, but stopped. She hadn't brought Vivian with the conscious thought of "Maybe she'll meet a nice man," but she couldn't deny that getting Vivian out of the house to meet other people had been a part of her motive. And to get her away from Carl, her father, for at least one evening.

"Am I that transparent?" she asked finally, not bothering to expand on her motives.

"Most people are," he said, "if you watch closely enough. Take myself, for instance. Take right now, this minute, for instance. You no doubt have noticed that I have drunk more than my father would prefer—more, perhaps, than you yourself would consider wise. From this you should have no trouble deducing that my father and I are not on the best of terms, and that he would be most gratified if I would 'settle down,' as he so often and so eloquently puts it. I, on the other hand . . ."

He shrugged eloquently. "Having been blessed—if that is the word—with more than sufficient trust funds and the like to allow me to do as I wish, I see no reason to do otherwise. No empire builder, I, but a simple conspicuous consumer."

"Who wouldn't be," Roslyn asked, "if he—or she—had the chance?"

"A lot of people, or so I am told by Father Benjamin. And, from my own personal experience, you. During our bookmobile trysts, I have not been able to ignore a certain—well, at risk of offending you with another cliché, a certain dedication. I have the definite impression that, even if you were to suddenly find yourself rich, you would continue in much the same way. Oh, you might buy yourself a new car, or a few comforts, or you might even start your own library, but you would still be plugging away in your attempts to awaken all the latent readers out there in the boonies."

Roslyn shrugged. "And you? It was your money that purchased the bookmobile. And you've been driving it for me, free of charge. Not to mention the driving lessons."

He laughed. "As I said, your friend Jenny is very persuasive. Besides, the family has a front to keep up. Last year it was a kidney dialysis setup for the hospital—first and only one in the county. And it cost a lot more than the bookmobile. As for driving, I hope you do not think I am doing it solely out of my love for children's literature."

Roslyn felt her face grow warm, but she forced a laugh and said, in mock astonishment, "You mean, sir, you have ulterior motives?"

"Of course. Doesn't everyone?" For a moment all the humor seemed to drain from his face. He glanced across the room, and his eyes settled briefly on his father, still standing near the foot of the wide, curving stairs.

"However," he went on, his voice becoming light again, his face resuming the half smile, "since we are speaking of people with dedication, I see that another of your kind is here tonight."

Paul took her arm and steered her past a half dozen groups and up to a pair of men standing near the door to the hall. One was young, probably in his late twenties, with a blond crew cut. Under his light blue jacket he wore a near black turtleneck. The other, older man was in his fifties, possibly sixty, his dark gray hair combed loosely straight back. His eyes were sharp behind old-fashioned, steel-rimmed spectacles, and he was virtually the only man in the room who wore a tie. Both men were of a height, about six feet, perhaps a little less. The younger man appeared slightly stockier.

"Roslyn," Paul said, indicating the older man, "this is one of the people who makes use of that dialysis machine. Through his patients, that is. Dr. Horace Macklin, perhaps the only doctor in the country who still makes occasional house calls. And this crew-cut anachronism next to him is his son, Eric. He also happens to be the Barton County sheriff. Off duty at the moment—or as off duty as a sheriff ever is. Gentlemen, may I present our new librarian, Miss Roslyn Stratton."

After a slight grimace in Paul's direction, Eric Macklin smiled at Roslyn and took her hand briefly. "I heard that Paul had donated some Blassingrame money to the library. I begin to see why. Very nice to meet you, Miss Stratton."

Dr. Macklin was frowning thoughtfully as he took her hand. "Stratton, he said your name was?"

"That's right."

"If you don't mind my asking, where are you from, Miss Stratton?"

"I just moved here from Wisconsin this week," she said.

"I see." Dr. Macklin nodded, but the thoughtful expression remained. "Very nice to meet you, Miss Stratton."

As he released her hand, his eyes shifted downward, as if to avoid her own gaze, and as he did, his thoughtful frown deepened abruptly and his eyes seemed to widen. For a second, then two, then ten, he remained silent, motionless.

"Doc, are you all right?" Paul touched the man's shoulder lightly.

Dr. Macklin started, his head bobbing up suddenly, his eyes darting from Paul to Roslyn.

"You said you were from Wisconsin," Macklin said finally, as if his lapse had never occurred, and both Paul and Macklin's son looked at him oddly.

"That's right," Roslyn agreed, vaguely embarrassed at the attention.

"Have you ever been in Fowler before?"

"Yes, but it was a long time ago." Her voice was barely audible over the general sound level in the huge room.

"When?" Dr. Macklin's voice was sharp, insistent.

"We left—my parents left when I was about a year old. Or so they tell me. This is the first time I've been in Fowler since. And I don't really—"

"And your parents? Alicia Stratton? Thomas Stratton?"

"That's right! But how did you know?"

"It's no mystery," Paul put in. "I'll bet he delivered you. He delivered practically everyone, even me."

Dr. Macklin was silent, and his eyes, pale behind his spectacles, seemed to glaze for a moment. He swallowed once, audibly, and then forced a laugh.

"Paul is right, of course," he said. "As he said, I delivered practically everyone. But tell me, how are your parents these days?"

"Mother is just fine. My father has been dead for several years."

Macklin blinked. "I'm sorry. I didn't know."

"There's nothing to be sorry about," Roslyn said, mouthing the standard reassurance, still feeling vaguely uncomfortable. "It's almost ancient history now. I was still in high school when it happened."

Macklin nodded slowly, distractedly. "I'm sorry, I really am. But you say your mother is all right?"

"She's fine. I'll tell her I met you the next time I talk to her. I've been trying to convince her that she should come to visit me for a few days once I get settled, but she hasn't seemed too enthusiastic over the possibility so far."

"Yes," Macklin said, his voice still sounding uncertain and distracted, "tell her I asked after her and that I hope to see her if she does come to visit you." He blinked again and looked around the room, absently searching. "We must talk again," he said, his voice suddenly formal, "but you must excuse me just now."

Macklin hurried away and, a moment later, Eric Macklin excused himself and left as well. Roslyn looked around to see Paul smiling bemusedly.

"And what was *that* all about?" she asked, more comfortable now that there were just the two of them.

"I don't know," he said, still smiling, "but you sure shook up Doc Macklin for some reason." Then he laughed aloud. "The way he asked about your parents, your mother— If I didn't know he was such a strait-laced old bastard, I'd suspect him of having a guilty conscience about something."

"For instance?"

"I'm not sure, but it does seem odd that he would be able to remember your parents' names, just like that. After all, he must have delivered thousands of babies."

"So? He could just have a good memory."

"True, and he probably does. But still, there was more to it than just remembering. He almost went into shock there for a minute." He shrugged. "I'll ask Dad, but I *think* Doc and his wife split up back about that time. Lots of years ago, anyway. Long enough ago that I don't remember it myself."

Roslyn frowned. "You're implying a connection? Between the breakup and my parents?"

"You know these small towns. Hotbeds of sin and all that."

Roslyn stiffened as it finally became clear what Paul was hinting at. "Him? And my mother? You're not serious!"

"You said it, I didn't. Besides, whatever it was, it's ancient history now, as you are wont to say. Unless your mother does come to visit you . . ."

"No!" Anger surged through her, but only for an instant. Then, abruptly, came a sinking feeling, a coldness that grasped at her stomach, driving out the anger. A coldness that told her:

It could be true!

As long as Roslyn could remember, her parents had, in one way or another, avoided discussing Fowler and their lives there. And not once in the twenty-plus years since they had moved, had they ever returned, even for a visit. It had been as if Fowler no longer existed. If Roslyn had not found the half dozen yellowed letters in a bureau drawer, she might never have known that she had an uncle and cousin still living in Fowler. When she had asked her mother about the letters, she had been scolded for "snooping" and had gotten almost no information. "Some relatives we haven't heard from in years," was all her mother would say.

But once Roslyn had found the letters, she hadn't been able to give it up. The faded letters, almost as old as Roslyn herself, had been like a voice from the past, and eventually she herself had written. It was Vivian who answered, not her father, and the letter had been an anticlimax, of course, not nearly as exciting as the mystery of the decade-old letters had been. Vivian and her father proved to be, just as her mother had said, some relatives they hadn't heard from in years. All that Roslyn really learned was that the reason they had not been heard from in all that time was that Roslyn's parents had never answered any of the letters, and soon the letters had stopped. Still, once the contact had been established, Roslyn and Vivian had maintained an occasional correspondence over the years.

When her father had died, Roslyn had assumed her mother would have called her brother to tell him, but she did not. By the time Roslyn realized that her mother had not called or even written Carl about the death, the funeral was long past.

Could Macklin have been the reason for such a total break between brother and sister? Could he have been the reason for their sudden departure from Fowler? Could her father have found out? Or been told by Carl?

No! It was impossible! It was all too tawdry, too much of a cliché to be true.

And yet . . .

Something had caused them to move nearly four hundred miles and never look back.

Something had hovered over them all those years, continuing even into the present, Roslyn realized. Her mother's uneasiness over Roslyn's going to Fowler to interview for the job, and the increased worry when Roslyn had told her she had gotten the job and would move to Fowler within a week . . .

"Roslyn? Are you all right?"

Roslyn came to herself with a start. Paul was leaning close, a hand on her shoulder.

"Yes, I'm fine," she said automatically.

"You faded out there for a minute, just like Horace did. I'm sorry if I said anything to upset you."

She shook her head. "No, that's all right. It just caught me off guard for a second. And it made me realize—I've been thinking the same sort of thing myself. I never admitted it to myself before, but I have been, for a long time. I've always wondered why my parents moved away from here so suddenly. And why neither of them would even talk about Fowler, ever. When you said that—well, this was just the first time I thought about it as—as specifically as that. The first time I thought of a specific person that my mother—or my father—might have been involved with."

Paul was frowning. "But I wasn't— Are you trying to tell me that my 'joke,' such as it was, might have had a grain of truth in it? I really *am* sorry. I never would have—"

"It's all right. It's about time I thought about it, out in the open. I'm twenty-two years old, and it's about time I admitted to myself that even parents are human. And that the 'stories' you hear about don't *always* happen to other families."

"Still, I'm sorry." Paul's voice seemed more sober now, his speech less slurred.

"I told you, it's all right!" She glanced around the room, looking for something or someone else to talk about. "Now, when do we get to meet the reason for this evening's festivities?" she asked, as her eyes came to the long, curving staircase, still vacant.

He blinked at the sudden change in subject. "Sophie?" He shrugged. "Any time now. She wants to be sure everyone is here before she makes her grand entrance. But she must not be due for a few minutes," he added, looking toward the stairs. "My father has deserted his post, I see, and he would never do that if her arrival were imminent."

Again Paul shrugged. "But I shouldn't allow myself to make light of his efforts. After all, my fate is not totally divorced from his. And I, for one, would certainly hate to have to learn how to earn a living at this late date in my life."

"You could always be a bookmobile driver," Roslyn said, smiling, glad to see the conversation returning to more normal channels.

"Perhaps." He looked around the room for a moment. "But I doubt that such an occupation could support me in the style to which I have always been accustomed."

There was a stir at one side of the room, toward the stairs, and they both looked around. At the head of the stairs, dressed in a striking dark green pantsuit, stood a woman. It could be no one but Sophie Blassingrame, Roslyn decided immediately. At this distance, her age was not obvious. The hair, a silvery, almost shiny, gray, was pulled back tightly, but somehow the elongated bun that was partially visible at the back of her head did not look old-fashioned.

For what seemed like at least a minute but was probably no more than a few seconds, she stood motionless, her eyes ranging over the crowd below her. Then, moving slowly but keeping her hands pointedly away from the banister, she started down.

Paul glanced around the room again, frowning. "Now where the hell did Father Benjamin disappear to?" He looked down at Roslyn, took her hand, and squeezed it briefly. "With the Number-one Blassingrame temporarily missing in action—or whatever—the second team had better step in. Excuse me a minute."

"Of course. If you—"

Before she could say more, he was gone, weaving quickly through the crowd, all of whom had by now turned their attention toward the stairs. Most of the conversations had died out as well. He met the old woman halfway down the stairs, and when she held out a hand, he took it and they continued the rest of the way together.

"Miss Stratton?"

Roslyn looked around sharply, startled at the voice that seemed only inches from her ear. Benjamin Blassingrame stood next to her, looking down at her.

She recovered herself and put on a weak smile. "Paul was just looking for you," she said.

He glanced toward the stairs, where Paul and Sophie had nearly reached the bottom. It seemed that everyone in the room was beginning a slow drift toward the stairs and Sophie Blassingrame.

"It won't hurt him to do escort duty for a while," Benjamin said flatly. "Lord knows, I've done it enough times."

He glanced down at her hand, in which she still held the empty glass her bacardi had been in. "But here, let me get you another drink."

"No, thank you, but—"

"No objections, Miss Stratton. Now, what is it you were drinking?"

"Bacardi," she said, acquiescing rather than arguing. "But I hope you can find a weaker one than the last."

"Of course. Just give me a moment and I'll prepare my own special mixture."

With a smile that seemed slightly out of place on his craggy face, he took her empty glass and was gone, moving rapidly toward a long table set up along one wall and covered with every imaginable kind of liquor. Ignoring the two tuxedoed bartenders, he moved up and down the table, locating and mixing and blending. Roslyn turned to watch the growing cluster around Sophie and Paul, and when she turned back, the elder Blassingrame was approaching her, a pair of glasses in his hands.

"I hope this is more to your taste," he said, handing her the glass from his left hand.

He lifted his own glass, held it toward her as if gesturing for a toast. "Your health," he said, then took a sip of his drink.

Roslyn smiled. She had never been toasted before that she could remember. "And yours," she said, raising her own glass to her lips and taking a small sip. She was, she realized, feeling very much relaxed.

"Better," she said. "That first one was a little too strong for me, although it does seem to be relaxing me pretty much. Actually, my taste normally runs more to soft drinks."

He nodded, glancing again toward the stairs, and Roslyn thought she could detect a slight nervousness in the motion. Paul was still visible over the crowd that clustered around them, but Sophie was completely out of sight even though, as Roslyn had noticed as Paul had taken her arm on the stairs, she was by no means short.

"There are times," Benjamin Blassingrame said, "when I wish my son's tastes ran in a similar vein to yours." He shrugged, a subdued version of the gesture his son used so often, and looked down at his own drink. "But, then, I have never set him that good an example, I'm afraid."

They were silent then, and Roslyn found her mind being pulled back to the discussion—if that was the word—of a few minutes before with Paul, and she remembered that he had said he would ask his father about Dr. Macklin.

"Mr. Blassingrame," she began, hesitantly, slightly startled at herself for even thinking about asking an almost total stranger the question she was working up to.

"Ben, please." His words had an automatic sound to them.

"Paul said you knew Dr. Macklin fairly well."

His eyes seemed to widen, but perhaps it was Roslyn's imagination. After a second, he nodded. "Yes, I've known Horace for several years."

"This may seem like an odd question, but Paul said you might know." She hesitated, beginning to doubt her ability to carry it through now that she had started.

"Yes?" Blassingrame's voice seemed less relaxed than it had before.

"According to Paul, Dr. Macklin and his wife separated about twenty years ago. He said you might know the exact date. At least the year."

He blinked and was silent for a moment. Finally, he nodded. "Yes, I remember. I've known Horace since we were in school together. But why . . . ?"

She shrugged self-consciously, realizing she was not quite as relaxed as she had thought a few moments before. "It's a little difficult to explain. You see, my parents left Fowler about that time, and—" She stopped. Suddenly, trying to explain it logically, the whole thing sounded ridiculous.

"And . . . ?" Blassingrame prompted.

"And—well, when Paul introduced me to Dr. Macklin, the doctor seemed nervous. And he remembered my parents immediately. He even knew their names before I mentioned them. As I said, I know this sounds silly, now that I think about it, but—well, my parents did move rather suddenly, and they've always acted as if Fowler didn't exist, or as if they wished it didn't. And it just occurred to me —or to Paul, really—that maybe my mother and Dr. Macklin . . ."

Suddenly, Blassingrame laughed. "An affair?"

She nodded. "I told you it sounds silly."

He stifled his laughter. "No, not silly. I never thought of Horace that way, though. It is possible, though, I suppose." He looked thoughtful for a moment, and his face became serious. "If it's true, would you like to know? Or . . . ?"

For a moment, the sinking feeling that had grasped her stomach when the thought had first come to her returned, but she forced it away. "Yes, I think I would."

"All right. As I say, I've known Horace for a long time, and . . ." He smiled at her confidentially. "I think I can find out. If you're really sure you want to know."

She nodded. "I do. It would explain a lot if it were true."

There was a burst of laughter from the group clustered around Sophie, and Roslyn turned toward them. And stopped.

For an instant, the room seemed to continue turning, and Roslyn blinked. The room steadied then, but her stomach . . .

At first she thought it was simply her nerves, returning again for whatever reason, making her stomach lurch. But no, she realized, this was something else. And there was a faint but growing feeling of nausea.

She shook her head, but it didn't help.

"Miss Stratton?" Blassingrame's hand was touching her shoulder. "Are you all right?"

Her voice came slowly. "I don't know. I feel—a little sick." She shook her head again. "It must have been that first drink. It was pretty strong, and I'm just not used to it. I think I'll be all right if I can sit down somewhere."

"Of course." Blassingrame took the glass from her hand and set it and his own on a small table nearby. Then he took her arm and, holding her firmly, walked her toward a door in the wall opposite the stairs. As she moved, the room again seemed to sway, and the nausea increased. They reached the door and went through into a small sitting room. As she lowered herself onto a couch along the far wall of the room, Blassingrame seating himself solicitously beside her, she felt weak. Blassingrame's square, rugged face loomed over her.

"Lie down if you feel like it," he urged. "I'll see if I can find Horace."

"No, I'm all right. I'm sure if—"

"Never you mind," Blassingrame said firmly. "You just lie still. I'll be back with the doctor in a minute."

She hated having people fuss over her, but when she tried to protest, she felt too weak to do more than slump down further on the couch. Blassingrame's huge form wavered as he stood up, towering nearly to the ceiling. She leaned back again, then sideways. She half slid down until she was lying on the couch, her legs still over the edge. With an effort, she lifted them onto the couch.

As if from a great distance, she heard the door close behind Blassingrame, and she was alone.

CHAPTER 5

It could have been a few seconds or a few minutes, Roslyn couldn't be sure, when the door opened again and someone entered the small room. She tried to sit up, but there was a hand on her shoulder, pressing her down.

"Just relax, Miss Stratton. Let me take a look at you."

She looked toward the voice. Dr. Macklin's face hovered over her, a strand of his graying hair falling forward, touching the frames of his spectacles. She could feel his hand on her wrist.

"Pulse about normal, I think," he said, after a few seconds. "Now, can you tell me just what the trouble is?"

"I don't know," Roslyn said, feeling helpless and a little foolish. "I felt dizzy, and a little sick. And I feel weak right now."

He nodded. "I see." His hand lay against her forehead. "You don't seem to have a fever." The hand went away and returned with a thermometer, which he shook and then stuck under her tongue. "Ben tells me you aren't used to drinking. True?"

She nodded weakly.

"Could be it, I suppose. Young Paul tends to make the drinks a little stronger than absolutely necessary."

After an impatient pause, he took the thermometer back, held it up to the light. "Slight temperature, but certainly nothing to worry about. Here, stick out your tongue."

She did, and he peered briefly into her mouth, then nodded. "Good enough."

Roslyn closed her mouth. "What is it?"

The doctor ran his fingers through his hair, pushing the errant strands roughly into place. "Could be the drinks, but I doubt it. There's been an odd little virus running around the county the last few weeks. In fact, Jenny Wellons at the library had it last week. It only lasts a day or so, sometimes less."

"You think that's what I have?"

"Probably. But if you're expecting any treatment . . ." He shrugged. "To tell the truth," he went on, his lined face breaking into a smile, "there's not much that can be done. Nothing that I know about, anyway. Just take it easy, take a couple of aspirin, go to bed, and stay there until you feel like getting up. It's that kind of virus."

Dr. Macklin looked up at Blassingrame, standing only a couple of feet away. "Anybody here that can take her home, Ben?"

"No," Roslyn spoke up, "I have my car. I can—"

Macklin shook his head, dislodging another strand of graying hair. "You'll be better off if somebody drives you. If it *is* this virus, it makes you a little dizzy at first. But you know that already, don't you?"

"I'm sure I can—"

Before she could protest further, the door burst open and Paul Blassingrame strode in. His brow creased in a frown as he saw Roslyn lying on the couch with Macklin standing over her.

"What the hell's going on? Are you all right, Ros?"

"It's nothing," Benjamin said hastily. "Just a virus, Horace says. I'm going to drive Miss Stratton home." He turned to Macklin. "Horace, you can follow me in her car. Then—"

"There's no need for that," Paul said. "In the first place, if anyone is going to drive her home, it's going to be me. In the second place, her cousin came with her and is currently having a fine time with Councilman Lory, so you had better leave the car here for *her* to get home in."

Without waiting for a reply, Paul turned his back on the two older men and sat down on the edge of the couch next to Roslyn. "How are you feeling? *Do* you want to go home?"

She smiled weakly. "I'm feeling a little better, but Dr. Macklin is probably right. I don't feel much like a party."

"Whatever you say. Bed and a little something to drink always—"

"No, thanks," she said, as the feeling of nausea became stronger for a moment, "no more to drink. To tell the truth, I think it was the drinks, not a virus. They were a little stronger than I'm used to. A lot stronger, as a matter of fact."

Paul laughed. "Just the opposite problem to my own. Most are too weak for my preference."

"Paul," his father said sharply, "you're in no condition to drive. You've had—"

"I've had quite a few, yes. But escorting Sophie—which I have been doing in your absence for several minutes now—can be a very sobering experience."

"This is hardly the time—" Benjamin began, but Paul cut him off again.

"Don't worry, Father, no more dirty linen in front of the guests. Now hadn't you better go look after Sophie? You know she likes to have someone on tap at all times. And in case you're interested, she was not all that happy with me as a last-minute substitute for the first team."

Benjamin stood silently, his eyes fixed on Paul, the muscles in his jaw tightening. Dr. Macklin, standing back from the couch now, looked at Benjamin nervously. Finally, the older Blassingrame's eyes shifted from Paul to Roslyn, and, with an effort, he seemed to relax slightly.

"Very well," he said finally, his voice still tight. "But you damned well drive carefully! And slowly! Do you understand me?"

"Don't worry, Father. If it will make you any happier, I'll even promise to fasten both seat belts." Though Paul's words were directed to his father, his eyes remained on Roslyn.

"Paul, I—" Roslyn began, but Paul cut the words off by lightly pressing his fingers to her lips.

"Don't worry about a thing," he said. "This is standard procedure for the Blassingrame clan. Don't think you're causing trouble. And now, if you will just lie quietly and rest for a couple of minutes, I will find Vivian and tell her that we're leaving. And that she can have the car for the rest of the evening. Although, the way she and the councilman were looking at each other . . ."

Paul stood up, looking at his father and Dr. Macklin. They stood facing him for several seconds, and then, with a brief glance at each other, the two older men turned and left the room.

Paul stood looking at the door, then turned back to Roslyn. The smile had reappeared on his face. He leaned down, took one of her hands in his, and squeezed it briefly.

"I'll be back in a couple of minutes," he said. "Just take it easy and don't worry about Father Benjamin. Or anyone else."

He straightened to his full height and, a moment later, the door was closing behind him.

Again, it could have been a minute or it could have been a half hour. When Roslyn opened her eyes, Paul was standing beside the couch, looking down at her.

"Feeling better?"

She thought for a moment, trying to come more fully awake. "I think so. I feel more tired than anything else. Or sleepy, maybe, I'm not sure."

She sat up slowly as Paul took her hands. She shook her head lightly and found that the room didn't spin any more.

"Yes, quite a bit better," she said. "But how long was I out?" She glanced at her watch.

"Only about ten minutes," Paul said. "You were resting so nicely, I didn't see any reason to disturb you."

Experimentally, she stood up. The room spun for a moment, and she swayed. Paul put his arm across her shoulders, holding her up easily.

"You know," she said as the room settled down, "I'm beginning to think that maybe I really couldn't drive myself home. Not safely, anyway."

"You'd better lie down again," Paul said. "After all, there's no great hurry about anything."

"No, I'm all right now," she said hurriedly. "I don't want to waste any more of your time than I have to. Besides, the way I feel, the sooner I can get to bed and to sleep, the better."

Paul hesitated, then shrugged. "You're no trouble, I assure you, and certainly not a waste of time. But, whatever you wish . . ." He took her hand and guided her toward a door, not the one they had entered through. "We can go out this way," he said, "and avoid the crowd. And it's a lot shorter."

The door opened on a narrow hallway that led directly to a side door of the house. A car, apparently Paul's, stood only a few yards away, and Paul helped her in. It was small but expensive-looking, very low to the ground, and even in the faint moonlight and the patches of light that came from the house windows, very yellow.

"The seat reclines," he said, as he climbed into the driver's seat, "if you want it to." He reached over and touched a lever at one corner of the seat, next to her right knee.

She shook her head. "No, thanks. But I will take the seat belt . . ."

He laughed and reached across her. After a few seconds of digging between the seat and the door, he located the belt, pulled it and the attached shoulder strap across her, and snapped them in place.

"Not the easiest thing to find. I guess it's part of the challenge of owning this kind of car, to be able to find the seat belts when they're fully retracted."

A moment later the engine roared into life, and the car began to move. She leaned back, half closing her eyes. The trees and the house lights moved past and then they were on the road.

True to his promise, Paul drove slowly and smoothly, and after a minute, Roslyn found herself slipping back into the same drowsy, half-awake state she had experienced on the couch. She closed her eyes and leaned her head back against the headrest. The only sounds were the steady rumble of the motor and the wind as it pushed through the window on Paul's side.

Slowly, she felt the last traces of consciousness drifting away, the sounds fading into the distance . . .

Suddenly, Roslyn's eyes snapped open, and she felt a tremor shiver through her body. The car slowed, and she felt Paul's hand on her arm.

"Are you all right?" His voice was full of concern.

Roslyn blinked and looked around. "I think so. I—yes, I'm all right. I must have dozed off for a minute and had a dream."

His hand remained on her arm for a moment, and she could feel his eyes on her in the near darkness. She glanced toward him, then beyond him at the trees and brush that lined the road. The car was almost at a stop, the headlights bathing the road ahead for several hundred feet but casting only heavy shadows to either side.

Ahead of the car, perhaps fifty yards down the road on the left side, was a narrow opening in the brush. Then, as the car began to move again, she saw that there was a gravel drive leading back among the trees.

"What's down there?" she asked, as they drew abreast of the drive. She could see nothing except that the drive curved away out of sight after a dozen yards.

Paul glanced toward the drive. "Just a cottage," he said. "A Blassingrame cottage, of course."

"You own this land?"

"Someday, maybe. Or are you speaking of Blassingrames generically, not specifically?"

She turned her head to look backward through the minuscule rear window of the car, and for an instant the view seemed to blur and shift. And—had that been a light somewhere back among the trees?

"Does anyone live there?" she asked.

"Not now. In fact, not for quite a while. We rent it out occasionally, but I don't think it's been occupied for several months now."

She watched through the rear window for another minute, until she could no longer tell where the driveway had been. Then, turning to face forward, she leaned back in the seat and once again closed her eyes.

But still, as the car moved on and she slowly drifted back into her half-dreaming, half-waking state, an image of the drive, curving back into the unknown blackness beyond her vision, continued to float eerily in her mind.

CHAPTER 6

Roslyn came awake suddenly but not completely. Her eyes snapped open immediately, but the near-darkened room, with only the faintest of moonlight filtering in through the lone window, did not register.

In those first moments, there were only the eyes—the impossible, fiery eyes that floated in the darkness before her. And the feeling of loss, as if the only thing that she loved—needed—was being torn from her.

Involuntarily, Roslyn's arms reached out, her hands grasping blindly at the empty air as the sheet and blanket were shoved aside, and she heard a distant moan.

Then, as her hands worked futilely in the empty air, the eyes faded into nothingness. The moan broke off sharply as she realized it was coming from her own throat.

Her arms flopped back onto the bed limply, and the faint outline of the room around her came into focus. The night stand, the bureau, the door to the hall, the closet, the faint rectangle of light that was the window . . .

She thought: That damned dream!

It had been several months since she had had it last, and she had just begun to think that perhaps it was gone for good. But here it was again, as strong and as ridiculous as ever.

She shook her head and rolled over in bed, squinted at the luminous dial of the clock next to the bed. Four o'clock, she saw. Well, nothing had changed. Moving four hundred miles hadn't changed the thing's schedule. Four o'clock . . .

But at least it was over for the night. That was the one nice thing about her particular dream: It never repeated. Once she had been awakened by it, she knew it would not be back, at least not on the same night.

But still, she had thought the damned thing was gone, that perhaps she had finally outgrown it, whatever the hell it was. It had been—when was the last time? Over a year ago, just before she had started her year of postgraduate work.

Well, once a year was better than the once-a-month schedule she had been on before.

Gradually, her memories of the dreams floating distantly in her mind, she drifted back to sleep.

When Roslyn awoke next, sunlight slanted through the window, and the odor of frying bacon filled the air. She threw the covers back and sat up quickly, and it was only as she was pulling on her robe and crossing the room toward the door that she remembered she had been ill the night before.

Whatever it had been, it was gone now, she realized. The quick motions she had made in getting out of bed had had no effect. There was no dizziness, and from the way her mouth watered at the bacon smell, she knew that whatever had upset her stomach was also gone.

In less than ten minutes, dressed in almost-matching green slacks and sweater, she was downstairs. Carl Jefferson sat in one of the kitchen chairs, engrossed in the sports section of the Sunday paper. Vivian was at the kitchen range, taking strips of bacon from a skillet and putting them to drain on a paper towel.

Vivian looked around as she caught sight of Roslyn out of the corner of her eye.

"Roslyn! Are you sure you should be up already?"

Carl looked up then. He nodded to Roslyn briefly, and then said, over his shoulder to Vivian, "Better put some more of that bacon in. Roslyn Stratton looks pretty hungry this morning."

Roslyn glanced at Carl, then moved past him and stood next to Vivian. "To tell the truth," Roslyn said, "that does smell pretty good to me. But let me do the rest. You sit down and—"

"Don't be foolish, Roslyn Stratton. She enjoys cooking. Don't you, Vivian?" Carl barely looked up from his paper as he spoke.

"Yes, that's all right," Vivian said hastily. "Just sit down, Roslyn. Do you feel all right?"

Roslyn looked from Carl to Vivian and realized there was no

point in insisting. She shrugged and moved to one side but remained standing.

"I feel perfectly all right this morning. Whatever I had seems to have gone away in even less than the twenty-four hours that Dr. Macklin promised. But a more interesting question—how did you and the councilman get along last night?"

Vivian looked down, concentrating on the skillet of bacon. "Pretty well," she said quietly.

"Councilman?" Carl looked up again, a wide-eyed smile on his face. "You didn't tell me anything about that. What councilman? What happened?" Despite the smile, there seemed to be a touch of harshness in the voice, Roslyn thought.

"It was nothing, Father," Vivian said, avoiding his eyes.

Roslyn frowned but said nothing.

"A councilman?" Carl persisted. "My Vivian and a councilman? Who was it?" He turned to Roslyn then. "Who was it, Roslyn Stratton? Or are you holding out on me, too?"

Roslyn glanced again at Vivian, who was still concentrating single-mindedly on the skillet. Roslyn took in a breath. "His name is Lory. From what little I saw, they got along very well."

Vivian looked up surreptitiously but said nothing.

"Well," Jefferson said, "very good. Very good indeed. I understand that Councilman Lory is a—is it a bachelor? Or divorced?"

"He was divorced, Father," Vivian said, her voice barely audible above the noise of the frying bacon. "His wife remarried last year, and she and her husband moved to California."

Carl looked up at Vivian in surprise. "My," he said, "you really *must* have gotten along well with him to have found all that out in one night. Do you think you'll be seeing him again?"

Vivian nodded as she took another strip of bacon from the skillet and laid it with the rest on the paper towels. Jefferson was looking at her thoughtfully when there was a knock on the back door.

When Jefferson made no move to get up from the table and answer the knock, Roslyn went. A startled-looking Paul Blassingrame stood just outside the outer door in the back yard. He was dressed slightly more sedately than usual, in well-pressed gray slacks and a Lincoln green knit shirt.

"Roslyn! Well, it looks as if Horace was even better than his word. A twelve-hour virus rather than a twenty-four. How are you feeling this morning?"

"Fine. No aftereffects at all, not even from the drinks." She stepped back from the door. "Won't you come in?"

"Thanks, but all I really came over for was to see how you were. And now that I know . . ." He shrugged. "Since you've recovered so nicely, maybe you'd like to go for a ride. After I left you last night, I got to thinking, and—but I won't tell you, I'll show you. If you want to come."

"Show me what?"

He laughed. "A surprise, let's say. And something that may solve at least one of your problems."

"Well, aren't you the mysterious one this morning," she said, matching his mood. "All right, I'll be happy to go for a ride—but not for a few minutes yet. Right this instant, I still feel as if I were starving, and Vivian is—" She stopped, thinking of Vivian and the bacon. And whatever else her cousin would have to fix. "Unless," she went on, thoughtfully, "you know of somewhere else that we could get a snack."

He shrugged, smiling smoothly. "Of course. Your wish is, as someone is reputed to have once said, my command. More or less."

"Good. Vivian has more than enough to do cooking for her father, without me adding to her load."

Paul's eyebrows raised a fraction. "Do I detect a certain hostility toward the elder Jefferson in your tone—again?"

"A little," she said. "Now you wait here and I'll be right back."

She hurried back into the kitchen, told Vivian not to bother with the rest of the bacon, got her purse from her room, and came back through the kitchen. She couldn't resist just one strip, and with an apologetic smile at Vivian, she grabbed one from the paper towel as she went past. She could feel Carl's eyes following her speculatively as she hurried through the back door.

In the daylight, the narrow driveway did not look as ominous as it had the night before, but Roslyn still had to suppress a faint shiver as Paul turned the car off the road into the shadows of the closely spaced oaks and elms that lined both sides of the drive. Ahead, the drive curved off to the right, then back to the left, and finally emerged into a clearing of sorts. In the center, shaded by three particularly large oaks, was the house. The cottage, Paul had called it, but to Roslyn it seemed as large as most houses she had lived in. There had to be at least four rooms, probably five or six.

The grass didn't look as if it had been mowed for several weeks, but it fit the surroundings. A close-cropped lawn, here, would look completely out of place. A hundred yards beyond the house, through the trees that closed in again on the other side of the clearing, Roslyn could see patches of a small lake.

She sat quietly as Paul got out and came around to her side of the car and opened the door. There was something about the house, the surroundings . . .

"Well, what do you think of it so far?" Paul asked.

She looked up, becoming aware of Paul standing by the open door, holding out his hand.

"Disappointed?" he asked.

"Not at all," she said, sliding out of the car. "It's very nice."

"I think so, too. Now, would you like to look around inside? Or have you decided to take it already, just on the basis of the beautiful surroundings?"

"Take it?" She looked at Paul, frowning. "I don't understand."

"You're looking for a place to live, correct?"

"Yes, but—"

"This is a place to live. A cottage, to be exact. Correct again?"

"It looks that way, but it also looks too expensive for my budget."

He shrugged. "Don't worry about it. Say a token payment of fifty a month and it's yours."

"Fifty a month?" Roslyn looked at him skeptically. "I assume there's a catch? Some fine print?"

Again he shrugged, smiling. "My, but librarians are suspicious. No, there's no fine print. And in case you're wondering, yes, it is worth considerably more than fifty a month. The last people who rented it—last summer—paid—well, just say 'much more.' But, then, they were not librarians."

"You have a special bargain rate for librarians?"

"For this one, at least. The one we were more or less responsible for bringing to Fowler."

She stood silently for a moment, looking at the house, the trees, the lake. It was nice, very nice, and there was that odd attraction she felt for it, but . . .

Finally, reluctantly, she shook her head. "I don't think so. I appreciate the gesture, but I don't think that's my kind of arrangement."

He laughed. "No arrangement, not unless you want it. Don't be so suspicious. Just think of it as a small, additional contribution to the library. And believe me, Father's accountants will find a way to make it look like that very thing." He shrugged. "Besides, it's bringing in absolutely nothing now. And in any event, it's no money out of my pocket, any more than the bookmobile was. It all comes from —who knows where it comes from? The accountants may know, but I certainly don't."

Roslyn turned to look into Paul's face. As always, a faint smile played about the lips, and the eyes, dark and deep-set, seemed distantly amused. For a moment, she wanted to pull back, to disengage before she got in over her depth. Despite the seeming ease with which she and Paul got along, the Blassingrames were more than a little rich for her blood. Maybe she would be better off adopting a little of Vivian's attitude.

But even so . . . She looked again at the house, feeling that same, odd tugging from some deep recess of her mind.

"All right," she said finally, going against her common sense, "on two conditions."

The look of amusement on Paul's face deepened. "Of course. And they are . . . ?"

"First, assuming the inside is anywhere as nice as it looks on the outside, I would pay a hundred a month instead of fifty. That's still not what it's worth, probably, but that's about what I was planning to pay for an apartment, so . . ."

"If you like." He shrugged. "I suppose I'll just have to take you out to dinner that much more often to make up the difference. And the second condition?"

"If—and it's a big if—if I can talk my cousin into moving out of her father's place, she can live with me."

His eyes widened briefly, but then he laughed aloud. "A chaperone? Well, why not? Certainly, you can have anyone you wish. Although I may draw the line if I hear that Councilman Lory has moved in, too."

"Not to worry," Roslyn said, feeling vaguely embarrassed and still not sure she had done the right thing. "Librarians are a very strait-laced lot. Hadn't you heard?"

"Rumors. Only rumors. And now, if you would care to see the inside?" He dug into his pocket for a key and led the way to the cottage's front door.

"At least take a look," Roslyn said, "and think about it. I really think it would be good for you to get away from here."

Vivian shook her head slowly. "I don't see how I could," she said, looking around Roslyn's room absently. "I really don't."

"If it's a matter of money, I'm sure—"

"No, that's not it. I could afford my half of the rent easily."

"Then what is it? Don't you think we could get along, living in the same house?"

"Of course that's not it!" Vivian looked up at Roslyn, a hurt look in her eyes. "How could you think anything like that? You know that I—"

Roslyn put a hand out, touching Vivian's shoulder lightly. "I know." She was silent a moment, bracing herself to continue. She knew why Vivian could not come—did not *think* she could come—but Roslyn had to see if she could get Vivian to admit it to herself.

"Then what is it, Viv? What's to keep you from moving in with me?"

Again Vivian shook her head. "It would be difficult for me, that's all."

Roslyn sighed. "Is it Carl? Is your father the reason?"

Vivian turned away and stood looking silently out the room's only window. Roslyn started to move toward her.

"Well, Vivian," Carl Jefferson's voice came sharply from the door, "*am* I the reason?"

Both women spun around to see Jefferson pushing the door open the rest of the way. He stepped part way inside and stopped. Anger flared up in Roslyn, but Vivian lowered her eyes and said nothing.

"Well?" Jefferson repeated, looking from one to the other. There was a thin smile on his lips, but his eyes were hard.

"Of course not," Vivian began. It seemed an effort for her to lift her eyes.

The anger in Roslyn fought with the feeling that, in truth, *she* was the intruder here, and she felt her nerves plucking at her stomach. But she had started it. She hadn't intended a confrontation like this, but it was here.

"All right, Mr. Jefferson," she said, forcing her voice to sound calm despite the tremors she felt all through her body, "as long as the question is out in the open, maybe we should talk about it. How long were you standing there?"

"Out in the open? I'm sure I don't know what you're talking

about, Roslyn Stratton. Do you have some kind of problem we should be talking about? As for how long I was standing there—" He shrugged. "Not long, just a few seconds. But, then, I didn't need to be standing there very long, now did I?"

Vivian, her eyes still downcast, hurriedly crossed the room and slipped past Jefferson. "It's getting late," she said almost inaudibly, as she passed him. "I'd better be starting supper pretty soon."

Jefferson turned his head to watch her as she went silently down the stairs. "You see," he said, returning his gaze to Roslyn, "there's no problem here. Or there wasn't until a week or so ago."

"Me, you mean?"

"Take it however you wish, Roslyn Stratton." His voice was hard and the smile had faded to almost nothing.

She looked past Jefferson toward the stairs. Faintly, she could hear Vivian opening and closing kitchen cabinets. She pulled in a breath, thinking: All right, I got myself into this, and I can't back down now. She could feel the perspiration forming under her arms, cold and icy.

"Your daughter can't be your servant forever. Don't you think she's entitled to a life of her own?"

He shrugged, and the remnants of the smile vanished altogether. "Vivian is hardly a prisoner. She can do as she pleases. She can go or stay as she pleases. She knows that."

"She does? What about school? I remember she was looking forward to college, really looking forward to it, but somehow she never made it. She stayed on here, instead."

"It was her decision, not mine."

"I'm sure it was." The words were clipped as she forced herself to go on. It was a struggle to keep her voice steady, to keep her eyes fixed on his face. "But I'm curious. Just what did you tell her that made her decide not to go? That was about the time her mother died, wasn't it? Did you use that? Did you talk her into waiting a semester? Until you were both over the effects of the death? And then another semester? And another?"

"As a matter of fact," Jefferson said, his voice now even harder, harsher than before, "that *was* when my wife died, Vivian's mother as you put it. And Vivian did not feel that that was the time to run away—to school or anywhere else. Not like my sister—*your* mother—ran."

Roslyn blinked. "*My* mother? What are you talking about?"

He laughed humorlessly. "She never told you, I suppose? How they ran from Fowler like thieves?"

Suddenly, Roslyn found herself on the defensive. "My parents moved from Fowler, yes. So?"

"Oh, I never blamed my sister, not for running. That wasn't her fault. Although I always thought that, after your father died, she might come back." He shrugged. "But she didn't. Apparently she never will."

"None of this is news to either of us," Roslyn said stiffly. "What are you getting at?"

"Getting at? Who said I was getting at anything? You're the one who's getting at things."

"What did you mean about my mother 'running away' from Fowler?" Somehow, Roslyn kept her tone aggressive, but it was becoming more difficult by the second. What Carl was hinting at came too close to what she herself had felt. What she and Paul Blassingrame had talked of the night before.

"You don't like the words, Roslyn Stratton? 'Run away'? Is that it? All right, pick whatever words you want. She left. She moved away. She didn't say a word to me. And for twenty years, I didn't hear a thing from her, not a word. Until Tom died, I figured it was just him. He wouldn't let her come back. But it's been—how long? Six years now? And she still hasn't so much as sent me a postcard. What would *you* think, Roslyn Stratton? Wouldn't you say she had 'run away'? And let me ask you something else, now that we're asking each other all these questions. Did she ever tell you anything about us? Did she ever say a word to you about me or Vivian? Or Claire, when she was alive?"

"No, but—"

"That's right, 'no'! Vivian tells me the only way you found out we even existed was those letters I wrote, back before I found out nobody was ever going to answer."

"There must have been a reason," Roslyn said, shaken as much now by the intensity of Jefferson's words as anything. "*Why* did they leave Fowler?"

Jefferson caught the new tone in her voice immediately, and the thin smile returned to his lips. "So you're in the dark, too, Roslyn Stratton? Aren't you?"

"All I know is, my father sold his business here and bought a new one in Hartland."

Jefferson shrugged. With Roslyn fully on the defensive, he seemed to relax once again. "So he did," he said. "What else is there to know?"

"But there must have been something. Didn't Mother even talk to you about it then? Didn't she tell you why they were leaving?"

He shook his head. "I barely saw her those last few weeks. And Tom . . ." His voice became softer, almost nostalgic. "You know, I used to like Tom. I really did. I knew him before he married your mother. We both grew up around Fowler. He was a couple of years behind me in school, but we—"

Jefferson stopped abruptly, shaking his head. "But he changed, Roslyn Stratton, he changed," Jefferson went on after a second. Some of the harshness had returned to his voice. "Those last few weeks before he sold out and moved, he changed."

Involuntarily, Roslyn thought: He found out. Her father had found out what was going on. *Had* it been Dr. Macklin? Or someone else . . . ?

"How did he change? Did something happen?"

Jefferson blinked, and his eyes focused on Roslyn again. "Did something happen? If I knew that . . . but I don't. He just changed. He was always mad about something—always! No matter what anyone said to him, he'd bite your head off. Business problems, he said. Maybe so, I don't know. I don't suppose I ever will."

Jefferson's features hardened again, and his voice became brittle. "But whatever it was, he had no business running off and taking your mother with him like that, without a word. Not even a simple good-by. One afternoon I saw him when I went past his shop. The next day, it was empty, and a week later someone tells me you've all moved away. Not one goddamned word to me! My own sister, and not one goddamned word!"

He fell silent, his face reddening.

"I've been trying to get her to visit me," Roslyn said lamely. "Maybe, now that I have a place of my own . . ."

He stared at her silently for several seconds, and then, as if he had not heard her words: "Not one goddamned word in more than twenty years! And now you want my daughter to run away, too!"

"She wouldn't be running away. She would only—"

"Call it what you want." His voice was choked, his face still red.

"What the hell do you want, Roslyn Stratton? What the hell do you want? Vivian's all I have left!"

Abruptly, his jaws clamping tightly shut, a mixture of anger and puzzlement on his face, he spun about and stalked out of the room and down the stairs.

CHAPTER 7

The first ring was barely completed when her mother's voice came over the wire.

"Roslyn? Is that you?"

"Yes, Mother, it's me. You must have been camping by the phone again, you answered so quickly."

"I was just watching TV. You know the phone is on the table next to my chair."

"I know, Mother, and you never miss the 'Sunday Night Movie.' How are you?"

"I'm fine, dear," and there seemed to Roslyn that there was a faint emphasis on the first word.

"I just wanted to let you know, you can come down any time, Mother. I found a house, complete with at least one guest room, all for you. And I'm moving in tonight. When can you come down?"

A hesitation, as Roslyn had known there would be. "I don't really know, dear. You know how hard it is for me to travel."

"I know how hard it is for you to travel to Fowler, yes. But if you don't want to drive all the way, you could drive to Milwaukee and take a plane to Indianapolis. I checked the schedule, and I could meet you at the airport. It's only an hour or so to Fowler from there."

Another hesitation. "I'll have to think about it. Are you still at Carl's now?"

"Yes, but Carl isn't here right now. Just Vivian. Would you like to talk to her?"

"No, there's no need for that. You're all right yourself? How is the job?"

"The job is just fine, and I'm just fine." She thought briefly of telling her that Carl was the only one who was not fine, and that maybe a reconciliation with his sister would help, but she restrained herself. She would save that for a later attempt, when she could call from the cottage, alone. "Incidentally, I met an old friend of yours. Dr. Macklin. Do you remember him?"

"Dr. Macklin? Yes, he was—he delivered you."

"That's what he said. He asked about you. He remembers you quite well."

"How is he? Is he still practicing?"

"Very much so. On me, in fact. He—"

"On you? What's wrong?" Alarm stiffened her mother's voice. "I thought you said—"

"It was nothing, Mother, nothing at all. Just a little virus—a twelve-hour virus, at that. I came down with it at a party, and he happened to be there, that's all."

"A party?"

"Yes, Mother, a party. A Blassingrame party. Do you remember anything about the Blassingrames?"

"Blassingrames?" A questioning echo. "They were—they owned a lot of property, didn't they?"

"They still do. And a lot of money." Roslyn went on to explain briefly the Blassingrame donation that had allowed the library to purchase the bookmobile. "For that matter," Roslyn concluded, "the house I'm renting belongs to the Blassingrames, too."

"It must be expensive."

"Not very. It's just a cottage. A large cottage, but still a cottage. It's out by a small lake, really nice." She glanced toward Vivian, who was working in the kitchen, making preparations for supper. "And I've been trying to convince Vivian she should move in with me. What do you think?"

"Does she want to leave Carl?"

Roslyn sighed. "No, but it might be a good idea if she did."

Another hesitation. "You might be right, but . . ." She was silent again, then spoke abruptly. "Do you know a woman named Hanneman?"

Roslyn blinked at the sudden change. "Frieda Hanneman?"

"Yes. Do you know her?"

"Slightly. I just met her last week. But how did you—"

"She called me yesterday."

"Called? Telephoned?"

"Yes."

"What about? What on earth did she want?"

"Nothing important. She said she knew you, and—" Mrs. Stratton stopped talking abruptly.

"And what?" Roslyn frowned, puzzled.

"Nothing important," her mother repeated.

"Did you know her when you lived here before?"

"I don't think so. But when did you say you were moving to your new place?"

"Tonight, this evening. But what about—"

"Will you have a telephone?"

"Extensions in practically every room, eventually, but not to-night. Paul—Paul Blassingrame; he's the one I rented it from—said he'd get it hooked up tomorrow. Now, Mother—"

"Tell Vivian hello for me. Now I really must hang up, before the bill gets too enormous."

"Mother, wait a minute!"

"I'll talk to you later, dear. Good-by."

"Mother! I—"

Roslyn stopped as she heard the click of the line disconnecting. For several seconds she stood listening silently, wondering what was going on. Her mother had always been odd when it came to discussing Fowler, but this sudden cutoff was strange even for her.

As Roslyn hung up, her mind went back to her brief meeting with Frieda Hanneman. She had thought at the time that the woman had seemed a little odd and that she had been unusually in-terested in Roslyn, but to make a long distance call all the way to Wisconsin to ask—what?

Whatever it had been, it had upset her mother—although Roslyn had to admit that it wouldn't take much to do that, not where Fowler was concerned. But maybe she should stop and see Mrs. Hanneman again, and try to find out just what the woman's interest in Roslyn and her mother really was . . .

CHAPTER 8

Roslyn opened her eyes sleepily, not sure where she was or why she had awakened. The bed was soft and comfortable, and her head was burrowed halfway into the pillow. There was almost no light, just barely enough to make out the window next to the bed.

Still not fully awake, she groped for the clock that should be on the stand beside the bed. Instead, her hand brushed against a wall.

For an instant there was surprise, and then she remembered. She was in the cottage. She had moved in yesterday, Sunday evening. She smiled in the darkness, not for any specific reason but simply from a feeling of comfort. It was the middle of the night, and she could let herself slide slowly, languidly back into the sleep from which she had not yet fully emerged.

She wriggled more deeply into the covers, pulling the blanket a fraction further over her shoulders. She closed her eyes again, and she imagined she could feel the bed slowly swaying as she drifted through a limbo that was not quite sleep and yet—

There was a sound.

Abruptly, her eyes snapped open and she was fully awake. There had been a sound, and it had been close by.

Slowly, she shifted her position beneath the covers, turning over so that she faced out into the room. Where had the sound come from? Probably just an animal of some kind outside the house, she told herself. After all, in an area like this, with woods all around, more than fifty yards from the road, a hundred yards from a lake, there would have to be animals.

Yes, that would have to be it. An animal, making an unfamiliar sound. Unfamiliar to her, at least. That was probably what had awakened her. She could sleep through the sounds made by cars and trains because she was used to them, but she had never before lived where there were animals—aside from an occasional dog or cat, of course. She would have to look around in the morning, and maybe ask Paul if he knew what kind of wildlife went with the house.

She lowered her head to the pillow again and started to burrow into it—and stopped.

Another sound, louder, and this time she recognized it. A door!

Suddenly, all thoughts of comfort were gone. All she could think was: Someone has broken in! Here I come to a crime-free country town and the first thing that happens, I get burglarized!

She thought of the phone, but in the darkness she couldn't see it. And what good would it do, anyway? She couldn't see to dial, and if she spoke into it . . .

She lay perfectly still. Burglars, she remembered from the police on TV shows and in books, were not looking for trouble, just for things to steal. If she was perfectly quiet, and he—they?—thought she was asleep . . .

But certainly he wouldn't come into the bedroom. He must know that someone was in here. He couldn't have missed seeing the car outside.

Another sound seemed to come from only inches away, and it was all she could do to keep from gasping aloud. It was the door to the bedroom. It was opening, a darker shadow in a room of shadows, moving slowly outward, toward her.

As she watched, every muscle tense, another shadow appeared and stood motionless in the door. Automatically, she squinted her eyes, trying to look as if she were asleep, even though, logically, she knew that the intruder couldn't see any better in the dark than she could.

For what seemed like an eternity, the new shadow stood silently, and Roslyn was sure that whoever it was could hear her own heart pounding, or at the very least, the uneven rasp of her breath.

Then the shadow moved. It detached itself from the door and moved the half dozen feet to the bureau and stopped.

Again it stood motionless and silent. Its back was to her now, she was sure, and she risked opening her eyes more widely.

What could he be after? How had he known someone had moved in here? It had been vacant for so long, and certainly there had been nothing here worth stealing while the house had been empty.

There was a faint click, and a muffled glow appeared, very faint, very indistinct, almost totally hidden by the bulk of the intruder. Then silence, and the shadowy bulk shifted as the glow moved slowly across the top of the bureau.

Still Roslyn held herself quiet, not even daring to shift her body, though she knew—logic again—that such motionlessness was itself unnatural. And the light, still hooded and indistinct, continued to move across the top of the bureau, then back. Whoever it was, she thought, as the shadow continued to waver before her, he was big. Or was it her imagination? Was it simply the darkness and her own terror that made the intruder seem so huge?

The form straightened and stood motionless, and the light vanished. Again the form was an indistinct shadow, only a few feet away.

Was he turning? Toward the bed?

She closed her eyes to slits, and even the shadows vanished. She could feel herself trembling, wondering how much longer she could keep control of herself. How much longer until she—

Without warning, something clattered to the floor. In the midst of the nerve-taut silence, it was thunderous, and Roslyn felt her entire body jerk with the sound. Her breath was sucked in with a gasp, but the instant that she realized what she was doing, she cut the sound off as sharply as with a knife.

At the same instant, an answering gasp came from the darkness only inches away, followed by an intolerable moment of further silence.

He knows I'm awake! she thought frantically, and automatically she drew back, shifting to the other side of the bed. The sound of her body moving under the crisp sheets was incredibly loud, drowning out the sound of her pounding heart. I should have grabbed the lamp, she thought, or the clock, anything from the table instead of—

The bedroom door slammed back against the wall, and retreating footsteps pounded across the living room floor. An instant later, another door swung noisily open, and there was the sound of running footsteps on the wooden porch, and a single thud as they hit the ground.

Then silence.

Slowly, Roslyn drew herself into a sitting position in the bed, still listening. But there was nothing. There was only silence, until—

In the distance, from the direction of the road, there was the sound of a car starting, and with a momentary squeal of tires, driving away.

Steeling herself, Roslyn reached out and turned on the bedside lamp. The sudden light stabbed at her eyes, and she closed them for a second, then opened them in a narrow squint. Gradually, the glare faded and she could see.

Nothing on the bureau seemed disturbed. The logical target, her purse, lay in plain sight, still closed. Her cosmetic case, open, sat near one end. A hairbrush lay against the case.

And on the floor, halfway between the bureau and the bed, lay—what? A small, black tube, but she didn't recognize it. It must be what he knocked off. Or dropped.

Taking a deep breath, she threw back the covers and managed to get out of bed. Automatically she smoothed down the half-length nightgown and slipped her feet into the slippers that sat next to the bed.

She leaned down to look at the tube on the floor. A tiny flashlight, she saw now. A penlight, probably single-cell. It was what he had been using to look at the bureau.

She reached for it but stopped. Fingerprints, she thought. She had seen enough movies to know that you didn't touch anything that might have fingerprints on it.

Enough movies . . .

Suddenly, standing in the middle of the room, she shivered. This hadn't been the movies. It had been real. There was the evidence of the reality lying on the floor in front of her.

She shivered again, not from the cold, and forced herself to sit calmly on the edge of the bed and pick up the phone.

CHAPTER 9

Eric Macklin stood in the door, looking into the bedroom, his back to Roslyn and the lone deputy who had originally come in answer to her call. Roslyn, in the jeans and blouse she had pulled on while she waited, sat scrunched into one corner of the couch in the middle of the room.

"So, as far as you can tell, nothing was taken?" Eric turned to face her, and once again she noticed the resemblance between Eric and his father, Dr. Horace Macklin. The same long, angular features, the prominent jaw, and the same heavy eyebrows, although Eric's nearly blond ones did not stand out as much as his father's darker ones. The longish crew cut, which looked as if he were in the process of letting it grow out, was slightly rumpled, as if he hadn't done more than run his fingers through it since the deputy's call had gotten him out of bed.

"Nothing, Sheriff," Roslyn said. "As I told you, now that I've had time to think about it, I imagine he was as scared as I was. The second I made any noise and he knew I was awake, he ran. And I do mean ran, not walked."

"But you're sure he already knew that you—or someone—was in here? He didn't act as if he thought the house was empty?" He sat down on the arm of a chair facing the couch.

"No, he was purposely trying to be quiet the whole time. And that light he was using—he shaded it somehow, maybe cupped it in his hand, I don't know. But he knew someone was here. And he *must* have seen my car parked outside when he came in."

Eric nodded. "Yes, it's all rather strange. It's as if he was waiting for you to move in. Or waiting for you to move out of your uncle's house, so he would have an easier time of it."

Roslyn frowned. "You make it sound as if he were after me, personally."

"It's possible. It could be a coincidence, of course. There are more of those running around than I care to even think about, but still . . ." He looked at her speculatively for a moment. "You have no idea what he could have been after?"

"None. I certainly don't have that much money. He should have been able to tell that just by looking at my car outside. Even in the dark, it is not impressive."

Eric smiled. "It's how old? Eight years?"

"Ten. With luck, I could trade it in for a couple of good tires. But it still runs all right, which is the important thing. Or so I keep telling myself."

"And you have nothing at all of value with you? Nothing at all?"

She shook her head, running her fingers through her uncombed hair. "I haven't even gotten my first check from the library."

He was silent for several seconds, then: "But you *were* at the Blassingrame party Saturday. That could make someone *think* you had something worth stealing."

She frowned again. "But you were there, too. Does attending a Blassingrame party automatically make you rich in the eyes of burglars?"

"In a way. It's not always true, of course. Witness your own case. And mine. But I was there because my father is an old friend of Benjamin's. And you went because . . . ? You're a new friend of Paul's?"

"That's right," she said defensively. "And before you go any further, yes, it was his idea that I rent this place. And I *am* renting it." As always when she went on the defensive, she realized, she had gone too far, talked too much.

A faint smile pulled at Eric's lips. "Did anyone suggest that you weren't?"

A hesitation, and a shrug.

"Not that I would blame you—or Paul—if you weren't," he went on. "But, then, that's hardly any of my business. Unless it relates to the break-in. Incidentally, who knew you had moved in here?"

"However many Blassingrames there are who live around here, I suppose," she said. "At least Paul and Benjamin, and according to Paul, an accountant or two."

"Anyone else?"

"Mrs. Sutherland at the library, and Jenny Wellons."

"That's all?"

She frowned. "I don't imagine the whole town knew it yet, if that's what you're getting at."

"Anyone else who might have been at the party Saturday night?"

She thought for a second. "Councilman Lory, probably. Vivian could have told him, if she's seen him since Sunday. But why this concentration on people at the party? You certainly don't think the burglar was *there*, do you?"

He shrugged, a more restrained gesture than Paul's elaborate motions. "Those parties get pretty big, and not everyone who gets in is always invited. Something that size, you always get a gate crasher or two."

"But a gate crasher wouldn't even know who I was."

"You're probably right. Just a coincidence. There are always a few burglaries. Not as many as in a large city, of course, but enough. More than enough. And as isolated as this cottage is, it's a perfect target."

"You don't think he'll be back, do you?"

"Not likely, but I *would* recommend locking your doors and windows. And I can have Sam here look in on you once or twice a night." He indicated the deputy, who was now standing by the front door. "He can at least keep an eye out for strange cars parked in your driveway."

He stood up and started for the door himself. Halfway there, he stopped and turned back to her. "What about people who came into the library? Anyone you've gotten to know? Anyone who would know you'd moved here?"

She shook her head, smiling. "You're determined to make it something more than a simple coincidence, aren't you? But no, there are several regular patrons I've gotten to know, but none who would know I've moved in here. And none, certainly, who would think I had anything worth stealing."

"No jewelry?" His eyes went to her hand. "What about your ring? I'm no expert, but it *looks* spectacular enough. Unusual, at least. And my father seemed rather taken with it at the party, to say the least."

"He was?"

"You didn't notice? When he first saw it, he almost went into a trance."

"Oh, when he— Is *that* what it was? I remember he seemed a little distracted, but I didn't realize it was the ring. Are you sure?"

"Reasonably. He was looking right at it. Or that's the way it seemed to me."

She held up her hand and looked at the ring thoughtfully. Mrs. Hanneman had asked her about it, and now Eric said that it was the ring that had gotten his father interested in her at the party.

"But you certainly can't think your father had anything to do with this!"

He laughed. "Not quite, but if he noticed it, then others must have as well, that's all. You didn't notice anyone else paying a lot of attention to it?"

She shook her head. "No one else at the party seemed to notice it at all. Compared to the jewelry most of the other women were wearing, it's probably pretty cheap."

"About how much?" he asked.

She looked at the ring again, frowning. "I don't really know. To tell the truth, the idea of price never came up before. I've had it so long, it's as if it were a part of me. I never even think about its being valuable."

"How much? A hundred?"

She shrugged. "Possibly. A jeweler once offered me that much, but that was a few years ago. But you certainly don't think . . ."

"As you said, you have nothing else that is of obvious value, nothing else to attract attention. And you also said that he was apparently searching your bureau, as if he were looking for something specific. He didn't bother your purse, which was sitting there in plain sight. If he had been after money, he would at least have opened it."

She looked at the ring again and, suddenly, a new shiver ran up her spine. For an instant, the gem's resemblance to a tiny eye was more pronounced than ever before. The flashing, reddish center, shifting endlessly in shape and shade, the multicolored surrounding area filled with translucent blues and greens and yellows . . .

She lowered her hand, looking away from the ring.

And the thought came to her: It was here, in Fowler, that I "found" the gem more than twenty years ago.

And then a further thought, accompanied by another shiver, this one deeper and longer lasting: Who had owned it before?

And why hadn't her parents ever been able to locate the owner?

"Is something wrong?" Eric Macklin's voice brought Roslyn sharply back to the present.

She shook her head sharply. "No, I'm all right. It's just that this ring . . ."

"Yes?" He moved a step closer.

"It's nothing, not really. It's just a little odd that you should mention it. It's always been something of a mystery itself, although I hadn't thought much about it until recently." Until Mrs. Hanneman asked me about it, she added to herself.

"A mystery? In what way?"

"A mystery in that I haven't the faintest idea where it came from. The opal, at least. According to my mother, I found it. Or it found me. It was here in Fowler, when I was only eight or ten months old."

"Only eight or ten months old? But how could you 'find' anything at that age?"

"That's part of the mystery. If anyone knows, they've never told me. It was while I was sick, during the flu epidemic here." She shrugged. "One day, there it was, clutched in my hot little hand, literally."

"Here in Fowler? Where, exactly?"

"Yes, here in Fowler, but I don't know where. I suppose it must have been somewhere in our house." She laughed. "I certainly wouldn't have gone crawling around outside in the street for it."

"No, probably not. But I remember the epidemic. It was the year I was in the first grade. We all got out of school for a couple of weeks. But if yours was a really bad case . . . Could you have been taken to a hospital? A lot of the people were, at least the really serious cases."

"I don't know. But I'll ask my mother the next time I talk to her."

Eric nodded. "And I'll ask my father. Maybe he remembers. He seemed to remember your parents pretty well."

"I'll be happy to hear anything you find out," Roslyn said, "but I can't imagine any of it having anything to do with the break-in, can you?"

"It probably doesn't. But you have to admit, it's interesting. But right now, we had better let you get some sleep. And I could use a little more myself." He moved back to the door. "Come down to the office if you think of anything more about the break-in. Or call me. Good night."

"And you call me if your father knows anything about the ring. All right?"

"All right." He lingered for a moment in the doorway, their eyes meeting, and then he was gone. The door closed behind him, and there was the sound of a car door slamming and an engine coming to life.

As the car pulled away and the sound faded, she looked once again at the ring. It couldn't possibly have anything to do with the break-in. It couldn't possibly . . .

CHAPTER 10

"Miss Stratton?" The male voice on the phone sounded familiar but Roslyn couldn't place it.

"Yes. Who is this?" She glanced at her watch as she spoke. She had been about to leave the house for the library when the phone had rung, and she didn't have much time to spare.

"This is Ben Blassingrame. I understand from the sheriff's office that you had a little trouble there last night."

"A little. Someone broke in. Or walked in. Sheriff Macklin tells me I left a window unlocked."

"But you weren't hurt, I understand."

"Not a scratch. My emotions got a little churned up at one point, but that was all. And nothing was taken, so there's no harm done."

"I'm glad to hear you're all right. If there's anything I can do for you . . ." His voice trailed off questioningly.

"Nothing that I can think of, but thank you anyway. And not just for the offer, but for everything else. Between the donation to the library and your renting me this house . . . well, I'm beginning to feel a bit indebted."

A faint laugh came over the line. "No need, I assure you. As I'm sure Paul has told you, the house had been vacant for some months and was bringing in absolutely nothing." He hesitated. "But there is something that you could do for me, Miss Stratton."

"Yes?"

Again he hesitated. "You see, in a way I feel responsible for what happened last night. After all, the house is mine, in a manner of speaking. And my son, from what he told me Sunday, almost twisted your arm to get you to take it."

"Don't be silly, Mr. Blassingrame. There was no way you—or he—

could have known someone would break in. It was just bad luck on my part."

"Even so, I can't help but feel a certain responsibility. It's common knowledge around Fowler that we own that particular house, and the mere fact that you moved in there might, in some people's minds, associate you with us."

"And with money?" Roslyn added impulsively. "Eric Macklin said something like that, too. He even thought that maybe, just because I was at your party Saturday and moved in here Sunday, someone thought I had something worth stealing."

Another hesitation, and Blassingrame said, "It's entirely possible. In any event, I do feel a certain responsibility. And you did say you became rather upset, so what I would like you to do is to stop in to see Horace—Dr. Macklin—sometime today."

She frowned puzzledly. "Dr. Macklin? But why? I told you, I'm perfectly all right."

"I know. I'm sure you are, but I would feel better if you went to see him anyway. Just to humor me, if you want to look at it that way. Experiences like that can be very upsetting to a person."

"It was nothing, really. I was just frightened for a minute. I think the burglar was more frightened than I was, the way he took off."

"I realize that, but still . . . As I say, I feel a certain responsibility, and I would rather take no chances that I can possibly avoid. Just consider it a favor to me."

Roslyn glanced at her watch again. If she didn't hurry, she would really be late. "I'll think about it," she said.

"That's all I ask. And so it won't take up any more of your time than necessary, I'm sure Dr. Macklin will be able to take you whenever you can find the time to drop in to his office. Or he could—"

"Thank you for your concern, Mr. Blassingrame, I'll think about it. But right now I'm almost late for work."

"Yes, of course. I understand. Good-by, then."

With a hasty good-by of her own, Roslyn hung up and hurried out the door. As she reached the car, she stopped and half ran back to the door of the house. With a self-conscious glance around the deserted yard and woods, she reached out and twisted at the door knob. Despite herself, she breathed a brief sigh of relief when she saw that it had, indeed, latched solidly.

Dr. Horace Macklin sat with his elbows on his desk, his fingers steepled so that they blocked half of his face from Roslyn's view.

"From these limited tests, Miss Stratton," he was saying, "you seem perfectly normal and healthy."

"That's what I told Mr. Blassingrame, but he insisted I see you anyway." Roslyn had finally decided to drop in on Dr. Macklin during her lunch hour, and he had been as good as Blassingrame's word. He had taken her directly into his office and had run through a quick battery of tests immediately. He had so obviously arranged his schedule for her convenience that it made her uncomfortable.

"I understand his viewpoint, I suppose," he said. "But as I was saying, for the most part you seem to be in perfect health. There is only one very minor discrepancy, which could very well be the result of what happened last night."

"Discrepancy? I thought you said—"

"Nothing serious, almost nothing at all. Your blood pressure is just a few points higher than I would like to see it. As I said, it could simply be a reaction to the excitement of last night. And the apprehension you will naturally feel, at least for a short while, that it might happen again."

Roslyn made a move to stand up. "In that case, since I passed with flying colors, I had better be getting back to the library. I've already taken more time than I intended."

"In a moment," Dr. Macklin said. "As I said, the elevated blood pressure is probably because of the tension you're under at the moment—the break-in, perhaps your new job, plus the fact that you have moved away from home for the first time—but I do think we should do something about it."

"But if it's not serious, and it's only temporary—"

"You never know, and it's always best to play it safe. What I can do is give you a shot. It should relieve some of the tension and lower the pressure. And then, if you could stop by for just a minute tonight before you go home, I could check the pressure again, just to be sure it's working."

Roslyn frowned doubtfully. "Do you really think it's necessary?"

Macklin smiled. "Not completely necessary, no. But I do think it's a good idea. It can't hurt, and there's a good chance that it *will* help. And since Ben is paying for all this, you might as well get as much good out of it as you can."

"All right," she said after another hesitation, "if you really think it will help me." She returned his smile. "After all, you were right about the twenty-four-hours-or-less virus the other day. It was gone by the time I woke up Sunday morning."

His smile faltered as he stood up, but it restored itself quickly. "Yes, I'm glad you recovered so quickly. You had a pretty light case of it, apparently. Now if you'll wait a few seconds, I'll get the apparatus for the shot." He shrugged apologetically as he went out the door. "My nurse is off on an errand, so I'll have to do it all myself this time."

She heard him moving around in the next room for a minute, then two minutes, and she glanced at her watch. If he didn't hurry up . . . She was already several minutes later than she had told Mrs. Sutherland she would be, and she didn't want to waste any more time than she absolutely had to. Not that the head librarian would be annoyed, but Roslyn had always hated it when she was unable to follow through on what she had promised. No matter what the reason, no matter how understanding the other people were, it still disturbed her. Her college roommate had often kidded her about it, and she herself knew that it wasn't totally reasonable, but—

Dr. Macklin reappeared in the door, a small hypodermic in one hand. "I don't know how good I am at this. I haven't gotten much practice lately. Maybe you'd prefer to wait until Jane gets back. She's so good at it, you can't feel a thing."

She shook her head. "No, it's getting late. I have to get back."

He nodded. "All right. Hold out your arm."

He took her arm, swabbed a spot with cotton, and then slid the needle into the chilled spot on her upper arm.

"Very smooth," she said, as he took the needle away. "If your nurse is better than that, she must be remarkable."

"Thank you. Now why don't you sit down for just a minute while I put this away. You might feel just a slight bit of dizziness for a few seconds, but that will be all."

"But you said—"

"It's nothing. If it happens at all, it will only last a minute. Then you'll be as good as new. Better."

"This won't affect me at work—"

"Not at all, not at all. Just sit down now for a minute or so. I'll be right back."

Again Macklin disappeared through the door, and she could hear his footsteps in the other room. She sat down and as she did she realized that, without her even knowing it, the dizziness had crept up on her. She shook her head, annoyed. He should have told her about that, not tricked her into getting the shot first. Again she glanced at her watch and swore under her breath. She would *really* be late now.

And, she thought, as her annoyance grew, she would be sleepy. The dizziness seemed to be going, but now her eyes were heavy, and it was all she could do to keep them open. She started to stand up, but Dr. Macklin appeared before her, his face concerned, urging her to stay seated for another minute.

"It affects a few people this way," he was saying apologetically, "but it's nothing to worry about. A perfectly normal reaction, and it will be over in another minute, I'm sure."

And it was.

Abruptly, her head was clear and she was no longer sleepy. She shook her head lightly and blinked at the suddenness. An instant ago, she had been ready to fall asleep, and now she was wide awake.

"You're feeling better now?" Dr. Macklin still stood before her.

"Yes, much better," she said. As if to prove it, she stood up quickly. "And I have to get back, right now."

"Of course." Macklin spoke as she moved past him to the other room. "Now don't forget, you're going to stop by for a couple of minutes this afternoon. All right?"

"All right, Doctor. About six o'clock, if that's all right. Now I really—"

"I'll be here."

She hurried through the empty reception room, and for an instant she wondered why there were no other patients. And the nurse was still not back from her errand.

Roslyn hurried on through the corridor and out onto Fowler's Main Street. Across the street was the courthouse, and as she glanced toward it, the clock in the tower struck once.

One o'clock, she thought, tilting her head up toward the dingy gray tower where two of the four faces of the clock were visible. It wouldn't be quite as bad as she thought if it was only one o'clock. Her watch must have been a couple of minutes fast when she—

Her step faltered as the clock faces registered in her mind. One-thirty? But it had been only a few minutes before one when—

She looked down at her watch as she quickened her pace, thinking it must have been slow, or even stopped. But no, it was almost the same, almost one-thirty.

She shook her head. She must have been in Macklin's office longer than she had thought. But she had just looked at her watch a few minutes before . . .

But it didn't make any difference. All that mattered right now was that she get back to the library before she lost even more time. She felt her stomach tighten at the thought of being this late.

But one-thirty! She must have looked at the sweep second hand on her watch, that was all. She had done it before, but she had always realized what she was doing in time to correct herself. She had never been this careless before.

She turned the corner, away from the courthouse, and she could see the library a block ahead of her. She walked as fast as she could without breaking into a run, and in a minute she was hurrying up the steps to the front door.

For an instant she hesitated, and the unbidden thought came: Such a depressing-looking building. You would think someone would come up with a better design than this. The library was, after all, supposed to attract people, not drive them away. And this one, with its bare, utilitarian exterior, looked like a blockhouse with glass doors.

Then, as she pushed through the doors, she realized that the interior was really no better. The walls and ceilings were a drab brown, and the rows of gray metal shelves were even worse. The fluorescent lights overhead seemed harsh and inhospitable, giving the entire building the look and feel of a barracks.

It was a far cry, she thought, from the Hartland library, where she had spent so many hours during her grade and high school years. There had been something about it—a friendliness, perhaps that this one did not have. Despite Jenny Wellons, who could make anyone feel at home in a matter of minutes, the Fowler library was a cold, aloof building.

And with the thought of Hartland, more memories forced themselves into Roslyn's mind. There was Mrs. Stuart, one of the library aides there. In some ways she had been not unlike Jenny Wellons. She hadn't been as old as Jenny, though she had certainly seemed old to the ten-year-old Roslyn, but she had been just as friendly and just as helpful—and just as eager to find books that she thought

Roslyn might enjoy. The head librarian, unfortunately, had not been as understanding as Mrs. Sutherland seemed to be, so Mrs. Stuart had been, Roslyn found out later, often under a cloud of disapproval. But it never seemed to bother her, any more than the same thing would bother Jenny. It had been through Mrs. Stuart, a tall, dark woman with short, reddish hair, that Roslyn had first become aware that there was more to a library than just books, that there was a whole world back there that she hadn't known about. Roslyn couldn't remember just how it had come about, but one day, when she was about twelve, she had been at the library just at closing time, and apparently on an impulse, Mrs. Stuart had invited her to look through all of the normally "out of bounds" parts of the building. Even now, ten years later, every step of the "tour" was vivid and fresh: Shelf after shelf of ancient, yellowing newspapers, bound into six-month volumes that were too heavy for either of them to lift alone; a table covered with new books that hadn't been marked and put out for circulation (she was even allowed to stamp a few of them herself!); stacks of battered and torn books waiting to be shipped out to be rebound; shelves and more shelves—more than there were upstairs in the main part of the library, Roslyn had been sure—of older, less popular books that had been taken from the main shelves to make way for the new books; the stacks of books waiting to be taken out to the bookmobile—or "library truck," which was what all the rural schools called it; the office that the librarians—

"Roslyn?"

Jenny Wellons' voice cut through her reverie like a knife, startling her back to awareness. Jenny stood in front of her, only inches away, looking up at her worriedly.

"Are you all right, Roslyn?" she asked, as Roslyn's eyes focused on her.

"Yes, I'm fine," Roslyn said hastily, and started to move past her, toward the office and check-out desk.

"You're sure?" Jenny persisted. "You came in through the front door, and then just stopped. It was like you—"

"I'm quite all right. I was just daydreaming for a second."

Jenny smiled uncertainly. "In the middle of the lobby?"

Roslyn forced a laugh. "I was reminded of something, that's all. The—the library in my home town. I hadn't noticed the—

resemblance before." She moved past Jenny. "And now I had better get back to work; I've already taken too much time."

"That's all right, I'm sure," Jenny said, following close behind Roslyn. "What did Horace have to say?"

Roslyn shrugged. "Nothing more than I expected. I'm perfectly all right, just a little nervous after last night."

Jenny nodded. "I don't blame you. I'd be more than just nervous, I can tell you. Now you're sure you're all right?"

"I'm sure. Now don't worry about me." Roslyn hurried past the check-out desk and back toward the stairs to the basement. Jenny, with a last look over her shoulder, returned to the desk, where a middle-aged woman was waiting impatiently with a half dozen books.

At the head of the stairs, Roslyn hesitated, and for just a moment, there came the touch of something that she could only think of as panic. For that instant, everything around her seemed alien and hostile—the building, the people, everything—and she felt a desperate longing for something familiar. A face, a hand, a room, anything that could break through this wall of isolation that she felt so suddenly and so strongly.

Harshly, Roslyn shook her head until she could feel her hair brushing at her forehead with the motion. Ridiculous! This was ridiculous, letting mere moods get such a grip on her!

With a visible effort, Roslyn threw back her head and started down the stairs, determined to dismiss the entire affair from her mind.

CHAPTER 11

Roslyn's mood had not improved by the end of the day. If anything, it had grown worse. Even Grommet, who had taken to leaving his window and spending much of his time trotting at her heels or sitting on her desk, hadn't cheered her up. Intellectually, she knew the mood was nonsense, but on this particular afternoon, her intellect seemed to have no control whatsoever over her emotions. It was, she told herself and Grommet a dozen times, nothing more than a case of belated homesickness. It was also a great deal like the depressions that descended on her on certain rainy nights, like the one that had given her so much trouble during those last miles of the trip to Fowler. There was no logical reason for it, but there it was. Once she left the stacks and offices in the basement and returned to the main floor, half the people who came in reminded her of people she had known in Hartland, and each reminder would, given half a chance, trigger another avalanche of nostalgic memories. The one thing that seemed to do more good than anything else was her own annoyance at herself for giving in to the mood, even temporarily, but it was cold comfort and produced problems of its own.

As she left the library that evening to walk the two blocks to Dr. Macklin's office, she surprised herself by thinking, seriously: Perhaps I *should* go back to Hartland, even if it's only for a visit.

And then she wondered: Could it have been that shot that Macklin gave me? Something to lower my blood pressure, he said, but could it have had side effects? But certainly he wouldn't give me something like that without telling me . . .

Suddenly there was a hand on her shoulder and she looked around, startled. Paul Blassingrame was keeping pace with her.

"Whither away?" he asked. "I was waiting by your car, but you crossed me up and headed this way."

"Sorry about that," she said, forcing herself to make an attempt at matching his easy, flip tone. "I have to see Dr. Macklin for a minute, and it hardly seemed worth driving and parking again just for two blocks. Not with a car like mine, at any rate."

His eyebrows raised as he looked down at her. "Dr. Macklin? What do you want with Horace? Did you have a relapse with your twelve-hour virus?"

"You hadn't heard? It's all your father's idea. After the break-in—you *did* hear about the burglar, didn't you?—he insisted, literally, that I let the doctor check me over."

Paul laughed. "A postburglary checkup? That's a new one on me."

"On me, too, but he insisted. And since he was paying the bill, and sounded as if he would send the doctor out to get me if I didn't agree to come in . . ."

He nodded sagely as they rounded the corner onto Main. "I see your point. Father is very hard to argue with. You either ignore him altogether or go along with him. And as long as he's paying for it, stick him for as much as possible. Get a complete physical." He laughed again. "What ever got something like that into his head, I wonder? Did he say?"

Roslyn shrugged. "I wondered myself, but all he said was that, since I was renting from the Blassingrames, he felt somehow responsible and didn't want to take any chances whatsoever. And that it would do his conscience good."

"I'm sure it would. And, since it is a medical expense, I'm sure he will find a way to deduct it from his taxes."

She shook her head. "You manage to be cynical about everything."

"Of course. It's the only way to be. The only alternative is to be a stuffed shirt. Or that seems to be *my* only alternative. I can't speak for you, of course."

"That's good." She looked up at him as they neared the entrance to the building containing Dr. Macklin's office. "Incidentally, I take it you had some reason for waiting for me?"

"Of course, but if you're going to take advantage of my father's generosity and have Dr. Horace give you a complete pawing over . . ."

"It's already done. At noon. I'll only be a minute now."

"He forgot something?"

She shook her head as Paul pushed open the door for her. "I guess the burglar and the rest of the excitement got on my nerves a little. My blood pressure was slightly high, and he gave me a shot for it. He wanted to check to see how it worked, I guess."

"Oh? Interesting. What was it he gave you?"

"He didn't say, but I'm beginning to think it was a downer of some kind. I've been downright maudlin all afternoon. I've even gotten to the point of thinking about chucking it all and going back home, to Hartland."

"You're not serious!"

She shrugged. "I don't know. Probably not. Or I probably won't be serious by tomorrow. Whatever this mood is, it can't last much longer. I hope."

"So do I, so do I! And I had better stick with you while you see Horace. We can't have him handing out things that get you to thinking such unthinkable thoughts as leaving Fowler."

"If you want to. He's just going to check my blood pressure, he said."

"I'll keep an eye on him anyway, just in case. You never know about these small-town doctors. Besides, he's a friend of Father's."

They stopped in front of the door to Macklin's outer office and Paul held it open for her. Dr. Macklin, sitting at the receptionist's desk glancing through a folder, looked up. A frown crossed his face as he saw Paul.

"Glad you could make it, Miss Stratton. Come right in." He stood up, motioning toward the open door to the inner office. "But, Paul, what are you doing here? Is something bothering you?"

"Depends on what you mean by bother. What Roslyn just said bothers me."

"Oh?" Macklin's eyes narrowed behind the steel-rimmed spectacles. "And what was that?"

"That she's thinking of leaving Fowler. I don't think she really means it, but . . ." Paul's voice trailed away into a shrug.

Macklin turned back to Roslyn. "Rather sudden, isn't it? It's not the break-in last night, is it? It's not frightening you away, certainly."

She shook her head. "I don't think so. But I don't really know just what it is. It's probably nothing more than a belated case of homesickness." She forced a smile. "I'll probably be over it by morning."

Macklin smiled professionally. "I daresay you will. I certainly hope so at any rate. Now, if you'll just step inside?"

She moved through the door, and before Macklin could follow, Paul slid through behind her. "Paul," Macklin began, "I don't think—"

"You're only going to take her blood pressure, right? That *is* all, isn't it?"

"Of course." Macklin's voice sounded annoyed, but then he fell silent for a moment, then shrugged. "If it's all right with Miss Stratton?"

Roslyn, too, shrugged. "It doesn't bother me."

The doctor began wrapping the pressure cuff around her arm.

"Incidentally, Ros," Paul said, as Macklin pumped the bulb and watched the mercury column slide up and down, "I've been out shopping for you."

She looked toward him, and her heart leaped. She was sure her blood pressure must have shot up several points as she saw the small pistol Paul had just taken from his jacket pocket.

"A thirty-two," he said. "Small enough for you to handle easily, and big enough to blast a rather untidy hole in any burglars that happen to get in its way."

"I don't think—" Roslyn began, but Macklin's sharp voice cut her off.

"Paul! Put that damned thing away! This is my office, not a shooting gallery!"

"Don't get your stethoscope in an uproar, Horace," Paul said, laughing. "It's not loaded. Not yet. How about it, Ros? Want a little protection?"

She shook her head sharply, and she could still feel her heart pounding. "No, thank you," she forced herself to say. "Just put it away, please."

Paul glanced from her to Macklin. "You, too?" He leaned forward, a half smile on his lips, the gun still lying loosely in his open palm. Then, as Roslyn drew back, her features tightening, Paul's eyebrows raised in a questioning look. "Are you all right, Ros? You look pale."

"I'm all right. Just put that away." She forced a nervous smile and added, half apologetically, "Guns make me nervous, I'm afraid."

"I can vouch for that," Dr. Macklin put in, his voice still irritated. "Her pulse just shot up at least thirty beats. Now damn it, Paul, put that thing away! Get rid of it!"

Paul glanced at Macklin, then back at Roslyn. He shrugged and dropped the gun casually into his jacket pocket, then lounged back against the wall. "About done, Horace? How's the blood pressure?"

"Just about normal, despite your fool antics," Macklin said, reaching out to remove the cuff.

"Good. No need for any more shots, then. Right, Horace?"

Macklin only nodded toward Paul as he spoke to Roslyn. "Now don't forget, Miss Stratton—feel free to call me at any time. If there's anything at all I can do for you . . ."

"I'll remember, and thank you," Roslyn said. Much of the tension caused by the gun had drained away, but she was still uncomfortably aware of the bulge in Paul's jacket pocket.

"Shall we go, then?" Paul straightened from his slouch against the wall and held out his hand to Roslyn. "What you need is a good, extravagant meal, and I know just the place to get one."

She held back, not taking his hand. "I think I'll go home instead. I have some reading to catch up on."

Paul grinned as he saw her eyes go involuntarily toward his pocket. "This still bothers you?" He patted the bulge made by the gun.

"A little. But I really do have to do some reading. I'm going to one of the schools tomorrow to talk to the kids, and I still have a few books to look over—books I'm going to talk about."

"But this—" Paul reached into the pocket, pulled out the gun, and quickly and casually, tossed it halfway across the room toward Dr. Macklin. "Catch, Horace."

Macklin jerked back, then made a frantic grab for the falling gun. He caught it clumsily, inches from the top of his desk.

"I don't want—" he began, but Paul's voice cut him off smoothly.

"Neither do we, apparently. If you can't use it, throw it away. Or donate it to our illustrious police department. Or the sheriff's department."

He took Roslyn by the arm then, and with a firm grip half propelled her out of the office and through the reception room. As

Roslyn glanced back, Macklin was laying the gun distastefully on his desk, frowning at Paul's retreating back.

"Now that we have that obstacle out of the way," Paul said, as they reached the sidewalk, "shall we be on our way?"

"I'm sorry, Paul," she said, trying to keep the annoyance out of her voice, "but I really don't have the time."

He sighed audibly. "I knew it as soon as I met you. Remember, I told you last week? You're one of those 'dedicated' types. Like Macklin and son. But didn't you say, just a few minutes ago, that you needed cheering up?"

"I'm not sure, but I think it was you who said I needed cheering up. In any event, I don't think an overpriced dinner in a dark restaurant would do the job." Especially not, she added to herself, if she were dragged there against her will.

Paul looked down at her as they walked. "You're serious, aren't you? You really *do* intend to go to your little cottage and spend the evening reading."

She nodded, faintly amused at the amazement in his voice. "I told you," she said, "I have to be prepared for the kids tomorrow."

"In that case, I assume you will at least be in the market for a bookmobile driver in the morning?"

She shook her head. "Not this time. This time I'm just going to one of the schools in town, to talk. They're close enough to the library—only a couple of blocks—they don't need a bookmobile. If I succeed in stirring their interest in literature, they can come to the library itself."

Paul sighed as they walked on. "Some days you just can't win." He eyed her profile speculatively. "From the tone of your voice, I take it that you wouldn't have the time or inclination for any other form of therapy tonight, either?"

She said nothing.

"I thought not," Paul commented after a few seconds, shrugging. "Well, I suppose I have no one to blame but myself. After all, I did insist that the cottage had no strings, and I did let you raise the rent on yourself."

The irritation flared once more in Roslyn. In all honesty, she had to admit that she had been expecting something like that, but she hadn't thought she would react so harshly. After all, she liked Paul well enough—or she had thought she did. But today, the way she had been feeling all afternoon, after the way he had gone ahead and gotten the gun for her without even asking, and the way he had . . .

"I can move out any time," she heard herself saying.

Paul held his hands up defensively. "No need, no need. Your virtue is safe as—as long as you want it to be."

A twinge of regret shot through her, not for her words but for the tone she now realized she had used. She had, she thought, sounded like something out of *East Lynne*. But before she could phrase a suitably noncommittal reply, Paul chuckled and squeezed her hand briefly.

"You know, Ros, you're turning out to be a new experience for me in more ways than one. In the first place, as I've pointed out on numerous occasions, I am not accustomed to dedicated people—at least none as attractive as you. And another thing I'm not accustomed to—" He shrugged, one of his more elaborate productions. "I don't want to shock you, but most of the girls around here—and even some who aren't from around here—are willing—nay, eager!—to leap into the sack with even the second in line to the Blassingrame fortune."

"You must have an interesting social life."

"It'll do." For an instant, as if a mask had slipped a fraction of an inch, there was a bleakness in his voice that seemed, strangely, to match the mood that had hovered over Roslyn most of the afternoon. But then it was gone, and the smile was back.

"It will definitely do," he went on, "until something better comes along. And I can't really say I'm holding my breath—or anything else—while I wait. In the meantime, if you don't want an 'overpriced meal' twenty-odd miles away, how about a cheapy about twenty-odd yards from here? In case you hadn't noticed, looming up on your right is the town cafeteria. For that matter, it's probably the only one in the county."

They stopped at the window, and Roslyn inspected the menu taped to the glass. "Why not?" she said after a moment. "But it's home to the books immediately after."

"Restriction noted," he said, as he held the door open for her.

The food, it turned out, was quite good, and Roslyn resolved to start eating lunch there and forego her usual brown bag for at least a few days. It would cost a little more but, she realized, she was getting tired of sandwiches and cottage cheese each day. And she was getting tired of packing them each morning, too. By the end of the meal, much of which had been eaten in silence, some of the afternoon's mood had dissipated, although she still felt it hovering in the background, as if waiting to pounce. Maybe she would call her mother again, take another shot at getting her to come for a visit. There had to be a way . . .

Then, for the first time that day, she remembered the last time she had talked to her mother, and she remembered what they had been talking about.

"Paul, do you know a woman named Hanneman?" she asked, as they stepped once again onto Fowler's Main Street.

"I thought you weren't the jealous type," he said, eying her skeptically, "and here you are, checking up on me already."

"Not that kind of a woman, Paul. She's in her fifties, and she owns that souvenir and doll shop just south of town. Remember I asked you about it last week?"

He thought for a moment. "I think so. With those wild-colored jobs in the window?"

"That's right. Do you know her?"

"I don't think so. What did you say the name was?"

"Hanneman. Frieda Hanneman. She says her mother and grandmother used to be pretty widely known in the doll world."

"Oh? In what way?"

"They made dolls, mostly for collectors, apparently. Wax primarily, and some ceramic. Expensive, at any rate."

He assumed a thoughtful frown. "Hanneman . . . I can't place the name offhand. But that doesn't mean anything. I can ask my father. Maybe he remembers. When did all this happen?"

"The dolls, you mean? I don't know for sure. Many years ago, I suppose."

"Dolls . . ." The frown he had assumed became genuine. "You don't happen to know what her mother's name was, do you?"

"No, why?"

"I very vaguely remember some old woman who used to come around the house when I was small, before I started to school, even. I don't know who she was, but for some reason I keep thinking she had something to do with dolls."

"Could you ask your father about it?"

He shrugged. "I don't see why not. But why the sudden interest in her?"

"Actually it's the other way around. She seems to have developed a sudden interest in me—or my family, at least. I stopped at her shop the other day, and when she heard my name was Stratton, she wanted to know about my parents. And then, apparently, she telephoned my mother last Saturday—long distance."

"Oh? What did she want?"

"I don't know. That's what bothers me a little. I talked to Mother Sunday, and she mentioned the call to me. But I couldn't get her to tell me anything about it. She just wanted to know if I knew anyone named Hanneman."

"Maybe you should call her back."

"I intend to, maybe this evening. That's what reminded me of this whole thing, the fact that I thought of calling her. But I don't think I'll get anything from her. She's had twenty years of practice at being closemouthed about Fowler." Roslyn frowned as she remembered some of the times. "It's as if she simply turns you off. Or as if she just didn't hear your questions. It used to bother me, the first few times I asked her anything. But I must have gotten used to it. This is the first time it's bothered me, at least lately." She shrugged. "But I'll take another shot at it this evening."

"How about a more direct approach?"

"Talk to Mrs. Hanneman, you mean? I intended to, but yesterday she wasn't in when I stopped by. And today, until now, I'd forgotten about it. Between the burglar and your father and Dr. Macklin—and my own crummy mood—I've been occupied with other things."

"How about right now?"

She thought for a second. "I might as well try stopping on my way home. If she's still not there, at least it's not out of my way."

"Mind if I tag along?"

"Feel free. As far as Mrs. Hanneman's, that is."

"Limitation understood," he said. "Some other time, perhaps."

"Perhaps."

"And perhaps someday you can even be persuaded to visit our own modest abode—sometime other than the annual party. You didn't get much of a chance to look around the last time, what with your sudden virus—or alcohol allergy, or whatever it really was. Who knows, you might even get to meet Sophie."

He chuckled, thinking of something. "You and Sophie should hit it off famously. If there is one thing she admires, it's ambition. Or perhaps I should say, the 'Puritan Ethic.' She's one of those anachronisms who believe that hard work is, intrinsically, good for you. Which may explain why she has a high opinion of my father and a low opinion of me."

"She sounds like quite a woman. I'd like to meet her sometime."

"Consider it done. It may take a day or two to work you into her schedule, but it shall be accomplished." He stopped and shook his head broadly. "I probably shouldn't be doing this, you realize. It will just make it three-to-one against me instead of two-to-one, the way it is now. You will undoubtedly join in when she and my father start another lecture on the virtues of work."

"You probably need it," Roslyn commented, as they approached her car behind the library and she saw Paul's yellow creation parked next to it. "Although," she added, "I rather doubt that it will do you any good. You look to be too far gone for simple lectures to reach you."

"Very perceptive. But I see that I was right. You haven't even met her, and already you're siding with her."

He shrugged again as she slid into her own car. He watched for a moment as the car ground into reluctant life and she pulled away. A minute later, he pulled onto the street behind her and followed close behind as she drove the mile from the library to Frieda Hanneman's shop. They both drove into the parking area next to the building.

"Looks closed," he commented, as they approached the door.

"It probably is," she said, glancing at her watch.

Paul reached the door before Roslyn, and after finding it locked, he knocked loudly, then listened. Roslyn, still standing by the display window, thought for a moment she glimpsed a movement inside, but no one came to the door.

"Nobody home," Paul said finally. "Want to try it again tomorrow? Or perhaps I could stop by, if you want me to?"

"No need. It's nothing important, I'm sure."

"As you wish." He came back down the steps and stood looking at her. "End of the line?"

She nodded. "For today, at least. Feel free to visit your bookmobile at any time, though."

He bowed slightly. "At your disposal, for whatever services you see fit to avail yourself of."

Chastely, a solemn smile on his face, he shook her hand and turned toward the cars. Roslyn remained on the walk in front of the display window, watching him as he got into his car, and with a subdued squeal of tires, pulled back onto the highway.

Roslyn looked back at the display window briefly, then turned to go herself. As she reached the Rambler, she heard a door open behind her, and the tinkle of the bell. A voice called to her: "Miss Stratton?"

She turned. Frieda Hanneman stood in the door, motioning for her to return.

"Can I do something for you?" the older woman asked as Roslyn approached.

"As a matter of fact, you probably can," Roslyn said, bracing herself and lunging directly to the point. "You could start by telling me why you called my mother long distance last Saturday."

"Come in, please. Come in." Mrs. Hanneman stood back, holding the door. Her face seemed slightly haggard and the tan slacks and blouse she was wearing were rumpled, as if she had been taking a nap. There were no lights on inside the shop, but the late afternoon sun, just barely above the line of trees on the opposite side of the highway, filled the room with a harsh, dreary light.

"My mother said you had telephoned her," Roslyn said.

There was another moment of silence before the dollmaker answered. "She didn't tell you why?"

"Just that you had called. Whatever it was, it seemed to have upset her."

"I'm sorry. I didn't mean to. It was just—"

"Just what?" Perhaps because of the mood that still hovered over her, perhaps because of all the questions her mother had avoided answering over the years, Roslyn's voice was harsh and demanding. Normally such a tone would have been impossible for her, but now it somehow seemed natural. "What was it you asked her? Or told her?"

Mrs. Hanneman was obviously uncomfortable. Her eyes lowered. "I wanted to know about when you lived here, in Fowler."

Abruptly, Roslyn laughed. "Did you find out anything?"

The woman frowned, puzzled at the sudden laughter. "Very little."

"It's no wonder. I've been trying to find out about that myself, with remarkable lack of success. But why? Why are *you* interested?"

Mrs. Hanneman hesitated, glancing toward the door. "That was Paul Blassingrame with you?"

Roslyn nodded. "It was. So? Do you have something to do with the Blassingrames?"

She shook her head. "No, not any more."

"You did at one time?"

Again the woman shook her head, more slowly. "In a way."

"But what does that have to do with—"

Abruptly, the woman turned and moved toward the door at the back of the room, behind the counters. "I will show you something."

"What—"

"Wait. I will have it in a minute." The voice came back through the open door.

From the workroom beyond the door, Roslyn heard the woman's footsteps for a second, followed by the sound of a cabinet door opening and closing. A few seconds later, Mrs. Hanneman reappeared, holding a small, red book. As she came closer, Roslyn could see that it was covered in a soft, dusty fabric of some kind, perhaps velvet. The cover, its corners rounded, was at least a quarter of an inch thick, and the pages, she could see, were of a heavy, dark material, almost as thick as cardboard.

The dollmaker laid the book on the counter, in the one remaining patch of sunlight. She opened it to a point three quarters of the way through.

Roslyn glanced at the woman's face, and then looked down at the open book.

For an instant, before her eyes focused fully on the picture mounted in the book, as a distorted image swam in her peripheral vision, a chill darted through her mind. For just an instant, before her mind took in the full picture, the glowing, fiery eyes that had haunted a hundred dreams leaped out at her from the photo.

CHAPTER 12

Roslyn blinked, and the rest of the picture came into focus. It was a doll, only a doll. It was delicately painted, the lips a realistic red, the face disconcertingly flesh-colored, and it was dressed in a red and white peasant dress. The detail seemed remarkable, as if it were a full-size dress that had somehow been reduced to this miniature size.

Yet it was the eyes that held Roslyn's attention, only the eyes . . .

"You have seen it before?" Mrs. Hanneman's voice penetrated to Roslyn's mind.

She shook her head and looked away from the picture. "No, never."

"You're positive?"

"I'm positive!"

Roslyn started to turn away, toward the door, but she stopped. She knew it was insane, but it was as if she could feel the eyes in the photo reaching out, watching her, sending tremors up her spine. Slowly, reluctantly, she turned and forced herself to look directly at the picture, forced her eyes to see it as it was, not as her mind had constructed it from that first brief glimpse.

And she saw that the eyes were not nearly as bright as they had seemed at first. They still glowed with an inner, multicolored light, but the fiery brilliance was no longer there. There were only the shifting shades of pink and violet and orange and green and . . .

The same shades that were in her . . .

Roslyn raised her left hand, turning it so that the opal ring was bathed in the fading rays of the sun.

"Do you recognize it now?"

Roslyn started at the voice, coming from only inches away. She looked toward the sound and saw the dollmaker's face, its hard lines softened in the dwindling light, the eyes searching Roslyn's own face.

"I don't know," Roslyn said, knowing that she lied even as she spoke. "It *looks* a little like the stone in my ring. But there must be a lot of stones like that."

The older woman shook her head. "There are many opals, yes, even many Australian fire opals. They aren't rare. But a stone of that particular shape . . ."

Pulling herself erect, Roslyn closed the book of photographs. "I don't understand. Is there some connection between the eyes of that doll and my ring?"

"What do *you* think?"

Roslyn frowned. "Is *that* why you called my mother? To find out about this ring?"

Mrs. Hanneman nodded. "It is one of the reasons. I was interested in what happened to you then, before you moved away. But she couldn't tell me anything."

A strange mixture of annoyance—both at Mrs. Hanneman and at her mother—and curiosity gripped Roslyn. "What is this all about?" she asked finally.

"I don't know. I had hoped that you—or your mother—could help."

"She probably could," Roslyn said, "if she would. But *you* have this picture. What is it? What is that doll? And what does it have to do with me? Or with my ring?"

The older woman hesitated before answering. "All I know for certain is that it is a doll my mother made a number of years ago. She kept photos of most of them here, in this book, taken before she delivered them."

"Then this doll was made for someone in particular? Who?" Roslyn's voice took on an intensity she hadn't fully intended.

Again, Mrs. Hanneman was slow in answering. "Her name was Jennifer Corson."

Roslyn's frown deepened. "Yes? Who was Jennifer Corson? Where is she now?"

The older woman's eyes seemed to cloud over then, and for a moment it was as if Roslyn were not there.

"Mrs. Hanneman?" Roslyn touched her lightly on the shoulder.

Mrs. Hanneman shook her head, and her eyes focused again.

"Where is she? Jennifer Corson is where she has been for the last twenty years. In her grave."

"Dead? I'm sorry, but—" Roslyn stopped, then began again, more deliberately. "No, I'm not sorry, not now. Twenty years is a long, long time ago. Who *was* Jennifer Corson?"

"No one."

"What do you mean, 'no one'?" Roslyn's voice was becoming sharper as the irritation grew. This was the same kind of reaction she had always gotten from her mother whenever she asked a question about Fowler, and it seemed a deliberate effort to frustrate her. "Now who *was* she?"

"She never had a chance to become someone." Mrs. Hanneman's voice was flat, but there was an intense emotion hidden just beneath the surface. "She was only ten months old when she died."

"All right. Her parents, then. Who are *they?*"

"They were dead before Jennifer was."

For several seconds, the two women stood facing each other silently. Then Roslyn remembered what she had thought that other time, the first time she had come into the shop: Mrs. Hanneman had lost someone in the flu epidemic twenty years before. Jennifer Corson? And the child's parents? Some of the irritation drained out of Roslyn, leaving her empty and hollow.

And then, into that emptiness, as if it had been hovering nearby, waiting, flowed the same undefinable bleakness that had plagued her most of the afternoon. But now it was stronger, more nearly irresistible, as if, during its temporary retreat, it had gathered its strength for this new assault. It seemed to dig more deeply into her mind, fastening itself more firmly, coloring everything she saw or thought.

"I'm sorry," Roslyn said. "I had better be going." Even the words were an effort, and as she spoke she realized that the sun had sunk below the line of trees on the opposite side of the highway. The entire shop was in deepening shadow.

Roslyn turned abruptly, not waiting for a reply. From somewhere came a touch of panic, and she could feel the shadows closing in as if they were physical things, and somehow they blended with the shadows in her mind. The dozens of dolls that lined the wall and filled the display cases seemed to stare at her with open hostility.

Roslyn pushed the door open and hurried outside. Behind her she heard Mrs. Hanneman saying her name, but she didn't stop until she was several yards from the door. The voice was still there, seeming to come from an impossible distance. She looked up at the tops of the trees beyond the parking area and could see the sunlight still touching them, but it gave her little comfort. It was a forlorn, lonely light, and even as she watched, it seemed to fade. The leaves moved slowly, and she could hear the same faint breeze that she felt against her face.

She turned and looked down the highway toward town, and the whole scene was alien to her—just as the library had seemed alien when she had entered it this afternoon. The view was familiar. She could recognize the road, the houses, and two or three hundred yards away, the junction of the two highways at the city limits, but she could not enter into it. She could not become a part of it. Everything was there, waiting to be touched, but she could not reach out and touch it.

"Are you all right, Miss Stratton?" It was Mrs. Hanneman's voice. She stood on the step outside the door to the shop.

Roslyn stared at her for a moment, hardly seeing her. She closed her eyes and took in a deep breath. Then, as she opened her eyes, she told herself firmly:

This is nonsense! It's just a weird form of homesickness, that's all, and I can lick it!

"I'm all right," she said, and she noticed that, surprisingly, her voice sounded normal. And then, as if dredging up a memory from the distant past, she recalled what she and the dollmaker had been speaking about—could it have been only minutes ago?

"I'll be talking to my mother again," she said, "probably tonight. If I can get anything out of her, I'll stop by again. And if you . . ."

Mrs. Hanneman nodded. "If I learn anything, I will let you know."

Abruptly, still moving in eerie isolation through an alien world, Roslyn turned and walked quickly to her car.

For a minute, then two, she sat in the car, letting it surround her like a rusting, ragged womb. It, at least, was familiar. It was something she could touch, something in which she felt safe and secure.

Even as the words occurred to her—safe and secure!—some inner corner of her mind laughed. Her eyes roamed over the dashboard, with its out-of-order oil gauge and clock, and her fingers automatically went to the biggest of the tears in the upholstery.

Safe and secure, indeed!

Again, more intensely, she wondered: What the *hell* is going on? What is happening to me? Could that burglar have unhinged me *this* much? Could Mother's continual evasions and "premonitions" about Fowler have affected me after all? Has my subconscious mind been storing all these things away, just waiting to dump them on me?

Or am I just cracking up? A new chill spread through her, not for any external reason, but at the terrifying thought that, somehow, for whatever reason, she might not have full control of her own mind. If *it* could betray her . . .

Violently, she shook her head, and a barely audible "No!" escaped from her lips.

She jammed the key into the ignition and twisted it sharply. It was a second after the engine caught that she forced herself to release it. She put the car into gear, and with the tires spitting gravel, pulled out of the parking lot.

She drove slowly, and it was nearly fifteen minutes later when she turned into the drive that led back to the cottage. It was on the south side of the road, and with the sun almost completely down now, the tree-lined drive looked as tunnel-like as it had the first night she had seen it.

For a moment, just after turning off the road, she slowed the car almost to a crawl. She half expected the feeling of aloneness and isolation to increase as she moved into the leafy tunnel, but it did not.

Then, with startling abruptness, the uneasiness and depression were gone. One moment they had been hanging over her like clouds, and the next moment they were gone. In the instant that she had applied the brakes to bring the car to a stop at the end of the drive, next to the cottage, the clouds vanished.

For several seconds after the car had come to a stop, Roslyn sat silently, looking around. The trees, instead of looming over her gloomily, rustled lightly in the breeze. The lake, barely visible in the distance, was cool and inviting, not cold and forbidding.

She shook her head sharply, a new fear brushing at her mind. The sudden departure of the feelings disturbed her as much as the feelings themselves. Sudden swings in mood, she knew, were not normal, and hers had been swinging like a pendulum all afternoon.

Or was she exaggerating the moods themselves? And overreacting?

Yes, that must be at least part of the trouble. No mood could be quite as bad as she seemed to remember hers as being, and—after all, it was only natural that she should become homesick at least once. It was just that her first—and only?—attack was timed rather oddly, that was all. There had been very little of it when she had first arrived, despite the rainy mood she had been in at first. It had just waited a week and a half to attack her, that was all. That, combined with the burglary, which was enough by itself to make anyone nervous . . .

And like the Saturday-night virus, the mood seemed to be gone now.

She got out of the car, and in a twilight that now seemed friendly and mellow, walked slowly to the cottage door.

CHAPTER 13

Roslyn's mother answered on the first ring. After the obligatory "How are you?" pleasantries were out of the way and the question of a visit to Fowler had again been side-stepped, Roslyn said:

"I talked to Mrs. Hanneman again."

"Oh?" In even that single syllable, Roslyn could detect an uneasiness.

"Yes. She showed me something, a picture. A picture of a doll."

"A doll? Why would she do that?"

"It had rather unusual eyes. They looked exactly like the opal in my ring."

A pause. "That's interesting."

"Yes, I thought it was, too. And she's a lot like you, Mother. She doesn't answer questions very well."

"I don't know what you mean. Haven't I always—"

"No, Mother, you haven't." A tinge of the annoyance Roslyn had felt before was returning. "Whenever I ask you anything about Fowler, you manage to change the subject. Now please, Mother, could you give me at least one or two straight answers?"

"Of course. I've never held anything back, you know that."

Roslyn sighed. "All right. Let's see, then. To start with, just *where* did I find that opal? You said it happened while I was sick, but . . ."

Another hesitation. "I don't really know. I've told you that. It just showed up in your hand one day."

"But *where?* Where was I when it appeared? Was I at home?"

The pause was even longer this time, and Roslyn was about to repeat the question when an answer came: "You were in the hospital."

"The Fowler hospital?"

"Of course. You had been very sick. Your fever had gone up to—" Abruptly, she stopped.

"Yes?" Roslyn prompted. "My fever?"

"It had gone up to over a hundred and three. Your father and I rushed you to the hospital that night. At first they didn't think you were going to make it." Her mother's voice was strained as she continued to speak. "We stayed at the hospital that entire night and most of the next day. It wasn't until that evening that your fever broke and they said you would be all right."

"And the opal?"

"It was in your hand the first time they let us in to see you. You were still a little delirious."

"But where could I have gotten it? Didn't anyone wonder? Didn't they try to find out?"

"The doctors did. But you seemed so attached to it . . ."

"They were never able to find the owner?"

"No."

"But it *had* to come from somewhere! From someone!"

There was a faint laugh on the line, strained. "I remember your father saying those very words. But wherever it came from, no one ever found out."

"The nurses? Could one of them have been wearing a ring? A necklace?"

"None of them ever claimed it. And the doctors said they asked everyone."

The doctors . . . "Who *were* the doctors? Was Dr. Macklin one of them?"

"Macklin? Why, yes, I think he was."

"Is that why he remembered you so well? From that time I was in the hospital?"

"I suppose it's possible. I don't know any other reason he should remember us."

"You never saw him otherwise? He wasn't a friend of yours? Or Father's?"

"We hardly knew him."

"But he did remember you very well. You and Father both. And he said he was the doctor who delivered me."

"Well, perhaps he did. But I still didn't know him except as a doctor."

"All right, Mother. Now what about Frieda Hanneman? Did you ever know her?"

"Did she say I did?"

"No, Mother. But she must have been very much interested in you to call you the way she did. And you never did tell me what it was she wanted."

"Nothing important." A hesitation. "Didn't she tell you herself? You said you talked to her."

"I told you, she's almost as bad as you are when it comes to answering questions. All I could get her to admit was that it had something to do with my ring. And with the time between then and when we moved to Hartland. She said you didn't tell her very much."

"There isn't much to tell."

"There's certainly more than you ever told me. Do you realize you've never even told me, really, why we moved away so suddenly?"

"But I have. Your father sold his print shop, and—"

"I know. But why? Why did he sell it? Why *then?* And why didn't you tell Carl about it? Did you know that he still resents it? The way you left without even talking to him?"

"But . . ." Her mother's voice faltered and trailed off after the one word.

"Look, Mother, why don't you come down for a visit. Seriously, I mean it. Maybe you could patch things up with Carl. It would do *you* good, and it would do Carl good, I think. And maybe it would even do Vivian some good. Carl got pretty upset Sunday, when I was about to move out, and he said a few things . . ." Roslyn pulled in a breath and continued. "This may just be amateur psychology, but I think one of the reasons he hangs onto Vivian so tightly is the way you and Father left. He feels—well, he thinks you ran out on him. Not because you left, but because of the *way* you left. And because you've never communicated with him since. And frankly, Mother, if you want my opinion, he has good reason to be upset."

"But you've always said that Vivian—"

"I don't mean he has good reason to hang onto Vivian the way he does. That's inexcusable, no matter what the reason. All I'm saying is that, *maybe,* if you make the first move to make up with Carl, it might help Vivian. Who knows, it might even help you."

"Help me? I don't know what you mean."

"Are you sure, Mother? Look, you've always been nervous about Fowler, as long as I can remember. You've never answered my questions about it. That information about my being in a hospital is the closest you've ever come to opening up with me. And since you found out I was going to be moving to Fowler to work, you've been worse than ever. Now I don't know what it is that's been bothering you all these years, but I do think there's a good chance that facing up to it, whatever it is, would help. And the best way to do that is to come for a visit. And don't tell me you can't get the time off. There's plenty of room for you to stay here. I even have an extra bedroom, so there's really no excuse now. None that you've ever told me about, anyway."

Again there was a nervous silence, and the moment her mother spoke, Roslyn recognized the tone. It was the same one she had used so many times in the past, and Roslyn knew that, whatever "breakthrough" had occurred when her mother had let out a few facts about her stay in the hospital, it was over now.

"I'll think about it," the voice said vaguely, and then hurried on. "But this call must be running up all kinds of charges."

"That's all right, Mother," Roslyn said, knowing the attempt was in vain. "Look, did something happen between you and Carl before you left? Or between Carl and my father? Are you afraid of him?" Roslyn almost winced at her own words, but she knew that half measures would do no good.

"Afraid? Of course not. Why should I be afraid of my own brother?" Her voice did not sound hurt, only puzzled and still a little remote.

"I don't know. But there has to be a reason for the way you've been acting. *Why* won't you come down for a visit?"

"Now, Roslyn, don't be upset. I told you, I'll think about it." Still remote, as if the words were being skimmed from some recording that had no real connection with the person herself.

"I know you told me that, and I know that you won't do it. Look, tomorrow I'll stop by to see Vivian, and I'll phone you from there. I'll get Carl on the phone somehow, and—"

"No!" For an instant, Roslyn could hear the panic surface in her mother's voice, and she relented.

"All right, Mother, I won't. Not now, not yet. But please, *think* about coming down for a visit. *Really* think about it."

"I will." The remoteness was back, the momentary panic subsided. Everything was back to "normal." A few more phrases, standard and meaningless, and the line was dead.

As she hung up, Roslyn wondered: What is it about Fowler that unhinges the Strattons so damned much? My mother refuses to even think about the place, and now I'm coming down with my own brand of weird behavior.

She laughed, thinking of the horror movies she had seen so often, wondering what sort of supernatural beast they would come up with to explain something like this. "What dreadful secret lurked beneath the surface of this seemingly normal midwestern town?"

Then the laughter faded, and once again she told herself her own problem was just an unusual and badly timed case of homesickness. But her mother? A family skeleton, no doubt.

But she would, she thought, stop to see Vivian and Carl tomorrow, and perhaps screw her courage up to the point where she could ask Carl a few direct questions. She was sure she wouldn't learn anything new and would probably end up getting into another argument with him, but at least she would be doing *something*.

CHAPTER 14

The ten o'clock news was talking quietly in the background when Roslyn saw the headlights of a car shine momentarily through the windows of the cottage. A moment later she heard the car roll to a stop on the gravel beside her own car. Looking out the window, she could see the silhouette of the bulky light attached to the roof of the car. The police?

As the door opened and the interior light blinked on, she saw that it was the sheriff, Eric Macklin. Puzzled, she went to the cottage door and opened it before he had a chance to knock. He was wearing the same tan zipper jacket he had worn the night before.

"Good evening, Sheriff," she greeted him, smiling. "Won't you come in? What brings you out here again?"

"I'm not disturbing you, am I? It is a little late."

"Not at all. I rarely get to bed before midnight, for one reason or another. Can I get you something? A soft drink? Coffee, if you're not in a hurry? Sorry I can't offer you anything stronger, but . . ." She shrugged. "As you may have heard from your father, I'm not much of a drinker."

"Neither am I. But no, thanks. I dropped by for a couple of reasons. First, have you thought of anything more about the break-in? Anything we missed last night?"

She thought for a moment. "Not really. But—you're sure you won't have anything?"

He grinned. "Just as I thought. You're a compulsive hostess. I still don't want anything to drink, but I will sit down if it makes you any more comfortable."

He looked at the stack of books at the end of the couch as he sat down and Roslyn dropped into a chair facing him.

"For my talk to the kiddies tomorrow," she volunteered, indicating the books.

He glanced at a couple of the titles, then settled back onto the couch. "You were saying? You said you didn't 'really' remember anything, and then went into a 'but.' What was the 'but' leading up to?"

"Nothing to do with this, I'm sure, but last night you wondered if someone might have been after this ring." She held up her hand briefly.

He nodded. "It still sounds like a reasonable guess. Certainly as good as any other. It *is* an unusual-looking ring."

"That's what everyone says. But this afternoon— Do you know Frieda Hanneman? The woman who runs the souvenir and doll shop at the south end of town?"

"Not very well, but I do know who she is. Why? Don't tell me she's interested in the ring, too?"

"Very much so, it seems." Roslyn went on to tell him about her visit to the shop that afternoon, but leaving out any remarks about her own, erratic moods.

"Jennifer Corson . . ." Eric repeated the name thoughtfully when Roslyn had finished. "The name is familiar, I know that, but . . . you say she died in that flu epidemic twenty years ago?"

"I think so, although Mrs. Hanneman didn't specifically mention flu."

"I'll ask Dad. If anyone could remember, it would be him. He's got a memory like an elephant. You saw how quickly he remembered your parents at the party Saturday."

"That's something else you can ask him about. I mentioned that to my mother when I talked to her, and she claims she barely knew of his existence. She said he was one of the doctors at the hospital when I was there with the flu, but that's the only time she remembers him. Except for when I was delivered, of course. But she was pretty nervous about it, even for her." She laughed. "But then, she's pretty nervous about anything that has to do with Fowler. Incidentally, speaking of your father's memory, did he remember to offer you that gun?"

"Gun? What gun?"

"Apparently he did forget. Paul Blassingrame picked a gun up today. He wanted me to take it, in case the 'burglar' returns. I didn't want it, so he left it with your father. Tossed it across the room to him, in fact."

"That sounds like Paul. But how did my father get involved in this?"

"I was in his office today," she explained, and went on to fill him in about Blassingrame's insistence that she be checked over.

"That's odd," he said, when she had finished. "He's usually not that generous. Or that concerned. In fact, as busy as he usually is, keeping track of all the Blassingrame business interests, I'm surprised he even knew about the burglary."

"I thought it was a little odd, too, but . . ." She shrugged. "I don't have any basis for comparison, never having met the man before last Saturday."

"And even that wasn't typical, from what little I know." Eric smiled, a toothy, amused sort of smile that Roslyn couldn't help but contrast to the smooth, almost professional smile that Paul Blassingrame specialized in. "The first time in recorded Blassingrame history that Sophie was kept waiting at the head of the stairs—and then escorted by someone besides Ben."

"Yes, I remember Paul was upset at the time, but Benjamin seemed to think it was about time Paul was initiated. As a matter of fact, Benjamin was talking to me about the time Paul was bringing Sophie down the stairs. He was quite calm about the whole thing. The only thing that seemed to upset him was a little later, when I got sick."

Eric nodded. "Dad told me you had to go home. He said it was a virus of some kind. But then, what isn't, these days?"

"Maybe a virus, and maybe some of the Blassingrame liquor. Paul gave me something that was pretty lethal, and I wasn't really used to it."

"Nobody is used to the kind of drinks that Paul hands out. He thinks everyone drinks the same way he does. Or should."

Roslyn shrugged. "To each his own, as the saying goes. He seems to be enjoying himself. And his money." She laughed then, and Eric responded with a questioning smile.

"Paul said the two of us should get along famously," she explained. "Two 'dedicated souls,' or words to that effect, he said."

His smile broadened, but he did not seem as amused as he had before. "Compared to Paul, I suppose, it's hard not to appear dedicated. But tell me, why does he consider *you* to be dedicated? Did you work ten minutes into your lunch hour once?"

"I don't know. The last time he mentioned it was this afternoon, when I told him I had to read a few books tonight to get ready for a talk to some kids tomorrow. He wanted to take me to an expensive restaurant somewhere out of town."

"The Blackford Inn, no doubt. It's practically outside the county, and it costs you the price of a meal just to get to a table. Very good, from what I hear. From Paul, among others. I've never tried it myself."

"We ended up at the Main Cafeteria," she said, and Eric laughed.

"More my style," he said. "And while I'm thinking about it, how about lunch there tomorrow? If you like roast beef, that's their specialty on Wednesdays."

"Fine," she said, wondering briefly why she didn't even hesitate. "I was planning to skip my brown bag tomorrow anyway."

"What time? Noon?"

"Make it twelve-thirty. We switch around, and it's Jenny's turn to eat early tomorrow."

"Jenny Wellons? How is she? I'm ashamed to admit I haven't been in the library very often lately."

"She's fine, but you can see that when you come in tomorrow. But tell me, why does Paul consider *you* to be dedicated? Did you arrest him for drunk driving once and refuse to accept a bribe?"

She had expected a laugh, but Eric's face remained sober. "Close enough," he said, but then a shadow of his smile reappeared. "I suppose the biggest puzzle to him is why I'm a sheriff when, according to Paul, I could be raking in money by practicing law, probably for the Blassingrames. I think it puzzles Benjamin a little, too."

"You're a lawyer?"

"More or less. I managed to make it through law school and came back here to practice."

"What happened? How did you get sidetracked into being a sheriff?"

He shrugged his broad shoulders. "Just lucky, I guess. I actually worked at the law business for a few months, even did a little trial work. Though in a small town that isn't all that thrilling. Or in a large town, for that matter, Perry Mason notwithstanding. Anyway,

I eventually had to take my turn as court-appointed attorney in a few cases—you know the ones, 'if you cannot afford one, an attorney will be provided without cost to you.' That was me. But I kept having run-ins with the police. More particularly the sheriff and his deputies, who were mostly his friends and relatives. Well, to make a long and boring story short and boring, after a few months of this, I took a little time off and signed on as a deputy. Just to see how the other half, the opposition, lived. And maybe to see if I could work up a little understanding for them, if not some sympathy. Unfortunately, it didn't work out that way. At that particular time, Barton County just happened to have one of the worst sheriffs in the state."

"Crooked, you mean?"

"Not exactly. Somehow he managed to stick to the letter of the law—if you happened to be someone he didn't care for. As for the others . . . it wasn't so much that he was crooked, although I'm sure he took in a few bucks under the table, he just liked the power. Anyway, after a couple of months of working with him and getting to know how it all worked, I decided I'd either have to practice law somewhere else or get someone else in as sheriff. As it turned out, an election was coming up in a few months, and he hadn't been fooling as many people as he thought."

Eric stopped talking for a moment and looked up at her. There was a trace of self-consciousness on his face. "So there you have it," he said. "The story of my life, such as it is. But tell me about yourself. How does someone decide to become a librarian?"

"I don't know about anyone else," Roslyn said, "but believe it or not, in my own case there's a certain parallel to the way you became sheriff."

His blond eyebrows raised. "You ran an older librarian out of town?"

"Not quite, but there are a few I wouldn't mind trying that on. Not anyone here in Fowler, but a few other places . . . No, what I meant was, when I was growing up I saw so many bad librarians that I—" She stopped for a moment. "You're sure you want to hear about this? You realize you may be listening to me lecture all night?"

He glanced at his watch. "I have no immediate appointments."

"All right," Roslyn said, grinning. "But don't say I didn't give you fair warning. Well, for whatever reason, I always liked to read, so I was always going to the library. And there was always some-one there who was trying to get me to read things that were 'good for me.' Most of the other kids I knew just quit going after a while. I might have, too, if I hadn't met one of the aides at the Hartland library. She was a lot like Jenny in some ways. I learned a lot from her—mostly what librarians *could* be like if they wanted to be. I guess I decided to get into the system and try to convert it from the inside. Although I don't think I ever consciously had any plans as grandiose-sounding as that. Does any of this make any sense?"

"As much sense as what I did, which may or may not be en-couraging to you. But what about Mrs. Sutherland? I don't know her very well, but she's always been 'the librarian' around here. And she's always seemed a little stuffy. Does this make her part of the enemy camp?"

Roslyn shook her head. "Under that exterior—according to Jenny, at least—she's really fairly open-minded as far as book selection and the rest go. She just tends to get a little nervous if someone starts complaining. But with Jenny—and now me—to back her up, she should do pretty well."

Roslyn leaned across from her chair toward the couch and pulled one of the books from the stack near one end. "I'm sure we'll get a few complaints about this one from the school, but she didn't object when I told her I wanted to take it tomorrow. In fact, Jenny says we've gotten a couple of objections already. But it's one of the most popular books we have, so it's one of the ones I'm going to talk about tomorrow."

She held the book up so Eric could see the cover, a montage of a dozen different movie monsters from the original Karloff Franken-stein to the colorful Japanese offspring of Godzilla and Rodan.

Eric took the book and started flipping through it. "Nobody ever recommended anything like this while I was in school," he said, grinning.

"Me neither," Roslyn said, "but I'll bet if they had, there'd be a lot more people reading and using the library than there are."

She reached for another book in the stack, a paperback. "Here's another that's pretty popular, but not necessarily 'good for the kids.' See what you think of this one."

It was an adaptation of a TV series, and obviously much used. "It's not very well done," Roslyn said, "but at least it's a step in the right direction. And who knows where it may eventually lead?"

He nodded, perhaps in agreement, as he continued glancing through the first book. After a minute he looked up. "If that offer of something to drink—soft—is still open . . . ?"

It was an hour later, after eleven-thirty, when he left.

"Oh yes," he said, turning back as Roslyn was about to close the door after him, "I almost forgot the other reason I came out here. I asked Sam—you remember, the deputy from last night—to look in on you now and then during the night. So don't be panicked if a car drives in here and turns around and goes right back out. It will just be Sam."

Roslyn frowned, her hand still resting on the door. "Do you think that's really necessary?"

"Necessary? No, not necessary. There's probably no real reason at all, but . . ." He shrugged. "Sam doesn't have much else to do on that shift. Do you mind?"

"Not at all. I appreciate the gesture, but I have to admit that the very fact that you thought of it at all makes me a little nervous."

"No need to be. Your average burglar doesn't pay a return call that soon."

"But last night you were hinting that it might not be your average burglar," Roslyn said. "He might have been after something specific, and if he didn't get it the first time . . ."

Her voice trailed off and her frown deepened. "You think he *will* be back, *don't* you?" she accused.

"Not really, especially if he sees Sam cruising by every so often."

"You're beginning to make me believe I should have taken Paul's offer of that gun." She shook her head. "Except it would probably be more dangerous to me—or Sam—than to a burglar."

"Don't worry about it. I'm sure nothing will happen."

"I was sure, too—until you mentioned Sam." Roslyn laughed shortly, to show she was not completely serious.

Eric smiled in return as he again turned toward his car. Roslyn watched through the open door as he climbed in, fastened the seat belt, and slowly pulled away and vanished into the tunnel leading to the road. After the lights were gone and the sound of the tires on the gravel of the drive had faded into silence, Roslyn stood listening at the door for a minute, feeling the chill night air drifting in. The only sounds were the breeze rustling invisibly through the trees and the high-pitched chirruping of a particularly noisy frog from the direction of the small lake.

She shivered once more as the wind momentarily gusted, and then, with a purposely steady, deliberate movement, she closed the door and fastened the chain. Then, one by one, she checked the latches on all the windows, and after rinsing out the glasses she and Eric had used, went to bed.

For the first time that Roslyn could remember, the dream was different.

As it always had, it began with the huge, looming forms, moving wraithlike around her like the ghosts of a race of giants.

The voices were the same—incomprehensible, cacophonous, unending—like an invisible tide that swept eternally through her brain.

The air was the same, thick miasma that refused to enter her lungs until she strained so hard that her muscles ached from the effort.

And the eyes, the fiery blue and green and violet eyes, were the same.

Yet it was different, for this time the eyes were embedded in a face, a huge, distorted face that seemed to be attached to one of the forms that swirled around her. A pale, painted face that, as the dream rushed on to its inevitable, terrifying end, seemed to somehow mirror her own . . .

CHAPTER 15

If asked, Roslyn could not have given a logical reason for stopping to see Mrs. Hanneman Wednesday morning. Perhaps she wanted to see if the same feeling of depression and panic would descend on her when she again entered the shop. Perhaps, after the strangely altered dream that had awakened her, gasping for breath, in the early hours of the morning, she wanted to see the photo of the doll once again, to reassure herself of its reality. Perhaps, even, she wanted to talk to the woman about the tiny bit of information she had gotten from the phone call to her mother. That, at least, was what she told herself when she approached the door to the shop shortly after eight-thirty.

"Come in, come in." Mrs. Hanneman looked closely at Roslyn as she stepped into the shop. "Are you all right? You seemed rather upset yesterday evening."

"I'm fine now. I don't really know what was the matter with me yesterday. I felt—well, 'strange' is as good a word as any. I felt it all afternoon, right up to the minute I got home."

"I was afraid the picture of the doll had . . ." Mrs. Hanneman's voice trailed off, and Roslyn saw that the red-bound book of photographs still lay on the counter.

Roslyn shook her head lightly. "It wasn't the picture, or anything else here. I don't really know what it was, unless maybe a very strange case of homesickness. That's what I've been telling myself, at any rate. But the reason I'm here—you wanted to know more about my ring."

"Yes?" Mrs. Hanneman's eyes fastened on Roslyn. "Have you learned something?"

"I talked to my mother last night, and—well, it isn't much, but she did tell me a little something. She said I was in the Fowler hospital for a few days, which is something she had never mentioned before. I knew that I had been pretty sick, but I hadn't realized it was that serious. She said my fever had shot up to over a hundred and three by the time they got me to the hospital. It took a day or so to get the fever to break, and—"

Roslyn hesitated, glancing down at her hand, at the ring that seemed more alive, more shimmering than ever this morning. "The first time my mother was allowed in to see me, I had the opal in my hand."

Roslyn looked up and was startled at the intensity of the other woman's gaze.

"But where did it come from?" Mrs. Hanneman asked. "Doesn't your mother have any idea?"

"I don't know," Roslyn said slowly. "If she does, she won't admit it. Or she hasn't yet. After yesterday, though, I'm beginning to have hopes that she'll open up more as time goes on." She laughed lightly. "Now that I've survived a full week and a half in Fowler, maybe she's beginning to loosen up."

"But in the hospital—*they* must have known where it came from!"

"If my mother has any ideas about it, she isn't admitting it, not yet. She says the doctors—one of them was Horace Macklin, by the way—inquired everywhere, but they couldn't turn up the owner."

Roslyn couldn't be sure, but she thought she saw a bitter smile cross Mrs. Hanneman's face, but it was gone before it could be fully realized.

"Dr. Macklin, you said? Perhaps you should ask him yourself," Mrs. Hanneman suggested. "Perhaps he remembers more than your mother does."

Roslyn nodded. "I've been thinking of that very thing, now that I know he was there. In fact, I'm beginning to wonder if that isn't why he remembers my parents so well after all these years. And he did notice my ring when we first met. Although he didn't say anything about it, just stared at it. But then, a lot of people seem to be noticing it lately. In fact, the sheriff has the notion that someone may have noticed the ring at the party Saturday night at the Blassingrames and decided it was valuable. At least he thinks that's one possibility to explain the break-in Monday night."

"Break-in?" Mrs. Hanneman's voice was startled.

"You didn't know? But then, there's no reason— I'm not even sure it was in the newspaper. In fact, I hope it wasn't. Someone broke into my house Monday night, while I was in bed, no less. When I woke up and made a noise, he ran. But from the way he acted, he must have been looking for something specific."

"The ring?"

Roslyn shrugged. "It sounded pretty farfetched at first, but I'm beginning to think it's possible. The break-in did happen just two days after the party, where a lot of people must have seen the ring —and according to Eric, those parties always have a few gate crashers. And it was just a day after I moved into the cottage."

"Cottage?"

Roslyn shook her head embarrassedly. "I'm sorry. I keep rattling on as if you should know what I'm talking about. I was staying with relatives until Sunday, and then I moved into a cottage three or four miles outside of town. A beautiful place, but pretty isolated."

"Southeast of town?" Mrs. Hanneman's voice was oddly flat, as if she were repeating something by rote. "About a mile this way from the Blassingrame house? A small lake in the back?"

Roslyn looked at her, startled. "As a matter of fact, yes. But how did you know?"

The older woman blinked once and pulled in a breath as if in an effort to collect her thoughts. "I don't know. I just felt . . ."

"But you obviously know of the cottage." Roslyn frowned at a sudden thought. "Is it a local landmark of some kind? Does it have a bad reputation? Is that why it was vacant, and they rented it to me so cheaply?"

Mrs. Hanneman shook her head. "Bad reputation? No, it's just that—" She stopped, her eyes lowered, then continued in a firmer tone. "Jennifer—Jennifer Corson—lived there most of her ten months."

"I'm sorry," Roslyn began, but then, remembering a similar scene from the day before, she went on in a different, less conciliatory tone. "You mentioned Jennifer Corson before, and her parents. Just who were they? Were they relatives of yours?"

Mrs. Hanneman was silent for a time, and Roslyn was about to repeat the question when she finally spoke, softly. "Yes, they were relatives. Jennifer's father was my brother."

"But what happened?"

"An auto accident. Edward and his wife were killed. Jennifer, their daughter, died less than two months later."

"You made that doll for her?"

Mrs. Hanneman nodded, her eyes going toward the book of photographs still lying on the counter. "Whenever a child was born in our family, we—my mother and grandmother, actually—made a special doll for it, using the child's birthstone for the eyes." She smiled weakly. "That's what comes of being a family of dollmakers for generations. Customs get started, and they're hard to stop."

"Jennifer was born in October?"

"October 10. Her birthstone was the opal. And you?"

"My birthday? July thirtieth. I'm afraid I could never afford a doll with eyes made from my birthstone. Rubies are a little too expensive for the Strattons." Roslyn glanced toward the book of photographs. "What happened to the doll? Do you still have it?"

The dollmaker was silent, as if trying to remember something that, for too long a time, she had tried only to forget. "It was buried with Jennifer," she said finally, a note of bitterness entering her voice. Her mouth moved stiffly as she spoke. "Or so I am told. The coffin was closed at the funeral."

"Closed? Why would that be? If she died from the effects of the flu . . ."

"I don't know why. It was decreed by—" She stopped, cutting the words off sharply.

"Yes? By whom?"

"By the wife's family."

"I don't understand," Roslyn said, frowning.

"I'm sure that I don't understand either." Mrs. Hanneman shrugged. "But it was a long time ago. And it was the last such doll that was made. When all three of them died within months of its being made . . ." Her voice trailed off, and her eyes seemed to fade into the past once more.

Roslyn stood silently for a moment, then reached over to open the book of photos. It fell open to Jennifer Corson's doll, like a book in which a favorite passage has been permanently marked by repeated usage. She studied it for a minute, then two. The face was the face she had seen in the dream last night, but there was more to it than that. There was a nagging sense of familiarity that Roslyn could not pin down.

"It was modeled on Jennifer's mother," Mrs. Hanneman said

quietly, breaking suddenly into Roslyn's reverie. "All the dolls were like that, modeled on one of the parents. My mother was really good at it—much better than I would ever be. If she had wanted, she could have been a sculptor."

"Yes," Roslyn said quietly, her eyes still on the photograph, "I can see that she must have been very good."

"The original form, the clay, had even more detail," Mrs. Hanneman went on, almost as if lecturing to herself. "But by the time the mold was made, and the final form, the wax form, made in the mold . . . Yes, she was very good."

After another lengthy silence, Roslyn glanced at her watch and closed the book. "I really have to be going," she said. "I'm due at the library in another ten minutes."

Mrs. Hanneman blinked. "Of course. Thank you for stopping in. I appreciate your thoughtfulness."

"It was nothing." Roslyn moved to the door. "If my mother lets anything else slip, I'll let you know. If you're still interested . . . ?"

"Thank you, yes. Very much interested." The older woman fell silent, but her lips remained slightly parted, as if she were about to say something but could not quite bring herself to begin. "Yes," she finally repeated, "I would appreciate it very much."

As Roslyn left, Mrs. Hanneman had turned back to the book of photos and was opening it slowly, almost reverently.

CHAPTER 16

It was about time for Roslyn's morning break when Jenny Wellons tapped her on the shoulder and pointed at the telephone in Mrs. Sutherland's empty office.

"It's for you, Ros, "she said.

Roslyn frowned puzzledly as she walked from the card catalogue to the phone. "Yes?" she said as she picked up the receiver.

"Ros? This is Paul. I have some bad news for you."

"Oh? You're resigning as bookmobile driver," she said, her tone deceptively light.

"Nothing as serious as that. It's just that your audience with the family matriarch, Sophie, will have to be put off for a while. She's—well, she says she's not feeling well enough to see anyone this evening, but frankly I think she's just a bit ticked off about last Saturday. What with the second team, namely me, escorting her down the stairs for her grand entrance. And then even the second team deserting her before the first team got back . . . Well, you know how it is."

"I can't say that meeting Sophie Blassingrame is my number-one priority, so I won't take great offense at the postponement. Or even the cancellation, if you have to cancel it. Besides, I think I'm going to stop in to see Viv this evening. And Carl. Maybe I can get something going after all these years."

"Get something going? Such as?"

Roslyn sighed. "It's a long story, and it gets longer every day. I'll tell you all the sordid details tomorrow. For right now, let's just say I hope that maybe I can at least get a start on a reconciliation between my mother and her brother. Or at least put a damper on a little of the ill feeling between them."

"Ill feeling? What is it, a family feud?"

"I told you, it's a long story. I think I told you some of it before, how my mother has always acted so strangely about Fowler, refusing to answer any questions about it. Well, she finally broke down and gave me a relatively straight answer, and—"

"That's good, but what was the question?"

"About this ring that everyone seems to be taking such an interest in. I've always known that I just 'found' it one day when I was a baby, but I never knew just where. Never even thought much about it until all the interest these last few days, particularly Mrs. Hanneman's."

"The doll-shop woman?"

"Yes. She even has a picture of a doll that her mother made several years ago for one of her relatives, with eyes made from opals that look a lot like the opal in my ring." Roslyn laughed. "From the way she acts, I almost get the feeling that she thinks my ring *is* one of the eyes. Although that's not very likely."

"Oh? Why is that?" Paul's voice was strangely quiet.

"She said the doll was buried with the girl it was made for." Roslyn's tone sobered now as she remembered Mrs. Hanneman's seeming bitterness.

"But you said your mother answered a question about the ring?"

"Nothing very informative, I'm afraid. After all this talk about it, I just realized that I never really knew where I had found the opal. So I asked her. She hemmed and hawed around for a minute and finally admitted that I had been in the Fowler hospital at the time. Which was news to me. I knew I had been pretty sick about that time, but no one had ever mentioned a hospital to me."

Paul was silent for several seconds. "Yes," he said finally, "there were quite a few that got into the hospital then. I was only eight or nine at the time, but I remember half my class in school was out. And I know that at least three or four were in the hospital for a few days. They even closed down the schools for a while. I don't think they ever figured out just exactly what it was—some off brand of flu, I understand, but it hit harder here than just about anywhere else."

He paused, as if switching his train of thought. "But the ring— you said you found it in the hospital?"

"Not the ring, just the opal. It must have fallen out of someone's ring, I suppose. Although how I ever got hold of it, I can't imagine. And apparently neither can anyone else. Mother said that the doctors checked with everyone imaginable to try to find the owner, but no one claimed it." She shook her head thoughtfully. "It's beginning to sound very mysterious, the more I hear of it. And I'm beginning to wonder if it isn't all tied in with the way my parents always avoided even talking about Fowler, let alone coming back for a visit."

"Yes, you told me about that. You have no idea why they were like that? They've never even hinted? No theories?"

"Not a one." Abruptly, sadness touched her, as it had the first night she had come to Fowler. "My father . . ."

"Yes? Your father did what?"

"I don't know. I'm trying to remember. When I found those letters from Carl, hidden away in a bureau drawer, he was furious, but only for a minute. And not at me for finding them, not really. It was more at Mother for having kept them. But it's a good thing she did. If she hadn't, I never would have even known Carl and Vivian existed."

Another silence as Roslyn stopped speaking. Then Paul, still quietly, said: "This girl you mentioned, a relative of the dollmaker —who did you say she was?"

"I don't know. A niece. The girl's father was Mrs. Hanneman's brother."

"But the name . . . ?"

"Jennifer Corson. Why? Do you know the name?"

"I remember there were some Corsons who lived here twenty years ago. But I think they all died."

"These did," Roslyn said. "It must have been very hard on Mrs. Hanneman. Though she never said anything directly, I got the feeling that she was very close to them, especially the little girl. Apparently the child's parents were killed in an auto accident only a couple of months before Jennifer herself died. And to make matters worse, the wife's family, for some obscure reason, managed to shut everyone else out. Mrs. Hanneman still sounds bitter about it. Not that I can blame her."

"How do you mean, shut out?"

"She didn't give me any details. It was mostly a feeling I got from her when she was talking about it. She seemed very bitter, even now. The only specific thing she mentioned was that Jennifer's mother's family insisted on a closed casket at the funeral. Which sounds a little strange for a child who died of natural causes."

"She thinks it may not have been natural?"

"I don't know, but . . ."

"You're sure it wasn't the parents they had the closed caskets for? Didn't you say they were killed in an auto crash?"

"Yes, but I'm sure she said it was Jennifer, the daughter. Although I suppose she could be getting things confused in her mind. She *has* acted a little strangely, come to think of it. And this thing has apparently been preying on her mind for the whole twenty years."

There was a brief silence, and when Paul spoke again, it was only to say good-by. His voice, even in those few words, seemed suddenly hurried and businesslike, and before Roslyn could reply, he had hung up.

She frowned at the receiver for a second, then hung it up and glanced at the clock beyond the check-out desk. It was time to get back to work, anyway. Her official "break time"—not that anyone paid much attention to such formalities, one way or the other—was about over, and it looked as if Jenny, who was trying to answer a question and check out some books at the same time, could use some help.

With a last glance at the phone, Roslyn hurried out of the office.

CHAPTER 17

Eric Macklin appeared promptly at twelve-thirty, and he and Roslyn walked the block and a half to the cafeteria.

"I asked Dad about that name you mentioned," he said, as they unloaded their trays onto a table near the window, "Jennifer Corson."

"Did he know the name?"

Eric reached over and took her tray and set them both on a vacant table. As he sat down opposite her, there was a faint frown on his face. "He *said* he didn't, but I'm not really sure."

"Not sure? Why not? Would he have any reason to lie?"

"I don't know. He's never lied to me before—so far as I know. But he seemed very surprised—even shaken—when I mentioned the name. He was almost as bad as when he saw your ring Saturday, but he recovered a little quicker."

"What *did* he say?"

"Very little. Just that he couldn't, offhand, remember the name. Then he wanted to know where I'd heard it."

"You told him about me and Mrs. Hanneman?"

He nodded. "That's another reason I wondered if he wasn't hiding something. He kept asking questions, even when I had told him the whole thing. If it were just a name he'd never heard of before, why would he be so curious?"

Roslyn finished off a piece of roast beef before answering. "He's beginning to sound like my mother. It's almost impossible to get a really straight answer from her, either. Although she may be improving a bit the last day or two."

They ate in silence for a minute, and then Eric's eyes searched the table. "Forgot the water," he said, standing up. "Back in a minute." He wended his way through the tables toward the water fountain and glasses near the rear, not far from the end of the serving line.

Roslyn glanced back toward the window and was surprised to see Paul Blassingrame striding by outside, heading for the door, his eyes fixed on her. A moment later, he had ducked under the railing that separated the dining area from the serving line and was standing next to her. He was wearing another wine-red outfit today, similar to the one he had worn the first day she had met him, but still different, and she wondered if he had a complete wardrobe for every day of the year. She couldn't help but contrast his clothes to her own, relatively conservative slacks and blouse.

"I thought you might be here." His voice had the same crisp tone it had had when he had talked to her on the phone a couple of hours earlier. "You'd better come with me."

She glanced down at her half-finished food. "We're not quite done eating yet."

He looked around sharply. "We?" Then he saw the other plate, and almost at the same time, Eric returned with the glasses of water.

"Well, good afternoon, Paul," Eric said, as he set the water on the table and resumed his seat. "Slumming again? Care to join us?"

Paul shook his head. He seemed slightly uncomfortable. "No, thanks, I've eaten. But Roslyn—" He stopped, his eyes shifting to Eric again. He leaned down next to Roslyn, putting his mouth next to her ear.

"Don't say anything to him," Paul whispered hastily, "or to anyone else, but meet me at Mrs. Hanneman's shop as soon as you can."

Her lips began to form a question but he rushed on, still whispering. "I said, don't say anything! Just meet me there. I think I may have solved your mystery."

Then, without another word, Paul straightened and walked away. He glanced back as he reached the door, and from his position behind Eric's back, held his finger to his lips in another plea for secrecy.

"What the hell was that all about?" Eric asked, as he looked sideways out the window and saw Paul moving purposefully across the street.

Roslyn started to explain and then, almost against her will, hesitated. After all, Paul didn't have any right to tell her what to do.

Especially he didn't have any right to ask her to lie. But his last words, "I may have solved your mystery . . ."

"Nothing serious," she said finally, uncomfortably. And then, to fill the uneasy silence: "I think he's jealous about last night."

"Last night? What about last night?"

"He must have found out you were at my place for a while, that's all. Remember I said I had turned down his offer of dinner."

"Then there *is* something between you two?"

Roslyn shook her head. "Not so you would notice. He's nice enough, usually, and amusing most of the time, but—" She forced a smile then in an effort to cover her discomfort. "I'm probably too 'dedicated' for him, anyway. Remember?"

"I remember. We're two dedicated people and we deserve each other. According to Paul, whose definitions of dedication and insanity are not all that far apart."

Eric looked directly at her then, and irrelevantly, she noticed that his eyes beneath the heavy blond brows were blue. And Paul's— She blinked, realizing she didn't know what color his eyes were.

"Be careful," Eric said, his voice quiet and sober. "Before you get in too deeply—" He stopped, shaking his head. "I'm sorry," he said, lowering his eyes, "I didn't mean to sound like a guardian."

"That's all right," she said automatically, her mind not fully taking in what he said. She glanced at her wrist watch without actually seeing the time, and she said: "I'd better hurry. I'm due back at one." She avoided his eyes as she spoke the lie and hurried ahead with the meal.

"Only a half hour for lunch?"

"Just today," she explained, still not looking up. "I've got a few things to get ready by one-thirty, and I didn't get as much done this morning as I thought I would."

He nodded and when she surreptitiously raised her eyes, she saw him looking back at her thoughtfully. But he said nothing, and Roslyn, feeling even more uncomfortable and wishing she had either told Eric the truth or said nothing at all, immersed herself in eating. Five minutes later, with another self-conscious glance at her watch, she excused herself and hurried out.

As she walked rapidly past the cafeteria window toward the library, out of the corner of her eye she could see Eric, his eyes following her with what seemed to be unusual intentness. She could feel her face burning and she swore under her breath at the sensation and at herself for having given in to the impulse to lie to Eric.

Damn Paul anyway! Just because he was in line to inherit whatever Sophie Blassingrame had, however much that might be, there was no reason she should give in to his whims that way. She should just turn around and go back to the cafeteria and explain to Eric. And apologize.

But Paul had said he had solved "her mystery" . . .

She swore again under her breath and quickened her pace even more, her long legs covering the ground as rapidly as any man's. Again she glanced at her watch, actually seeing it this time, unlike those times in the cafeteria. Twelve fifty-five, which gave her a good twenty minutes until her forty-five-minute lunch break was over. Five minutes or less to drive to the shop, five minutes back, which left her ten minutes for Paul to explain his "solution" and for her to tell him off for his high-handed behavior.

Behind the library, she got into her car, and instead of going back up Eighth to Main—which would have meant coming within a dozen yards of the cafeteria—she drove through the alley to Ninth and crossed over to Main from there.

At the shop, she parked at the back of the parking area, as far away from the highway as possible. To keep the car in the shade of one of the trees, she told herself, but she knew it wasn't true. Paul's yellow status symbol was nowhere in sight, and she wondered if he were hiding it somewhere, too, or if he had just decided not to wait for her.

But he and Mrs. Hanneman were both waiting inside the shop. Neither was talking as she entered, and both looked toward her sharply.

"All right, Paul, what the hell is this all about?" Roslyn asked.

"Did you tell Macklin where you were going?" Paul asked.

"No! Damn it, Paul, you—"

A smile flickered in his eyes. "I'm sorry. I should have known. Dedication and honesty often go hand in hand, so to speak, and you had a hell of a time not telling him the total truth. Right?"

"That's close enough for the time being!" For once, his references to her "dedication" didn't amuse her. "Now are you going to tell me what's going on, or—"

"Just listen to what Frieda has to say. You won't be sorry you came."

Roslyn looked from one to the other. Mrs. Hanneman looked uncomfortable. Her hands were clasped in front of her, moving nervously over each other.

"Tell her," Paul prompted the older woman, "who Jennifer Corson's mother really was."

Mrs. Hanneman's eyes went to Paul, then back to Roslyn. "Her name was Ruth. Ruth Blassingrame."

Roslyn frowned. "Blassingrame? As in—" She glanced toward Paul. "As in Benjamin and Paul Blassingrame?"

Paul nodded, seeming to take over from Mrs. Hanneman. "Sophie's daughter. Which would make Jennifer my second cousin, or maybe third. I can never keep those things straight. It's sort of complicated, but what it amounts to is, if Jennifer had lived, she would have been in line to inherit the bulk of the estate. Most of which my father will now inherit one of these years."

An odd feeling stirred in the pit of Roslyn's stomach. "You're not saying that Jennifer was killed. Are you?"

"No," Paul said, "we're pretty sure she wasn't. Although," he went on, seeming to turn the thought over in his mind, "I suppose it's possible that her parents were. But we'll never know now, not after all these years. It's easy enough to tamper with a car."

The feeling in Roslyn's stomach grew stronger, a sinking, hollow feeling. "But what does this have to do with *me?*" Without knowing exactly why, she knew that she was afraid of the answer, the same way her mother had always been afraid of answers dealing with Fowler . . .

"Show her the picture of the doll again," Paul said to Mrs. Hanneman.

Her face now rigidly under control, the dollmaker moved stiffly to pick up the red-bound volume of pictures. As it had before, it fell open to the desired page, and she held it out to Roslyn. Mrs. Hanneman said nothing, but her eyes were fastened on Roslyn's face.

"Does it look familiar?" Paul asked.

Roslyn looked at it. The eyes seemed to expand as she watched, to glow as they always had in her dreams . . .

"The eyes," she said, "are just like my ring. But that's nothing new. I saw that yesterday." Her voice still reflected some of the remaining irritation with Paul.

"Not the eyes, Ros," he said, "the face. Look at the face."

Reluctantly, Roslyn looked back at the photo, trying to blot out the eyes that still seemed to dominate the face so completely. It was not the typical doll's face, not a bland expressionless child's face, but almost an adult face. And not really a beautiful face, although the hair, light brown and loosely curled over the entire head, was most attractive. The face itself was slightly angular, the lips full, the nose just slightly larger than perhaps it should have been, and . . .

The dream last night? The oddly altered dream? But that was only natural. She had seen the doll for the first time yesterday evening, and she had naturally included it in the dream. But that meant nothing.

She shook her head. "It seems familiar, somehow, but it must be because of the eyes, and that damned dream I've always had."

"Dream?" Paul's eyes widened and his voice was sharp.

Roslyn explained, briefly, about the dream that had haunted her for so long. When she had finished, Paul was smiling, and Mrs. Hanneman's face seemed tenser than ever, as if she were about to lose control totally if she allowed herself to slip for even an instant.

Paul looked around for a moment, then leaned down next to Mrs. Hanneman, and whispered something in her ear. She nodded stiffly and hurried from the room.

"What the hell is going on?" Roslyn asked, much of her irritation bubbling back to the surface at Paul's action. "Do you whisper orders to everyone?"

"Be patient a second," Paul said. "You'll see."

Then Mrs. Hanneman was back, carrying a round, dressing table mirror. She held it out to Roslyn.

"Look in it," Paul said.

"What the—"

"Just look in it," he repeated, "please."

Grudgingly, she complied, and as she did, Paul reached out and took the book from her hand. After a second, he held it up next to the mirror so that the photo and Roslyn's reflection were next to each other.

Involuntarily, Roslyn gasped.

"You see it, then?" Paul asked. "You see the resemblance?"

"But why—I don't understand!" Roslyn lowered the mirror abruptly, almost dropping it on the counter. The irritation vanished, suddenly replaced by the uncertain beginnings of panic.

"Are you sure you don't understand, Roslyn?" Paul went on. "That doll, remember, was modeled after Ruth Corson—Ruth Blassingrame. Jennifer's mother. And now you tell us that you've dreamed of that doll—its eyes, at least—most of your life . . ."

Suddenly, it was as if the world had turned upside down. The room spun around Roslyn and she braced herself against the counter. Paul's hands were on her shoulders.

The words came slowly, haltingly. "You're saying I'm *not* Roslyn Stratton? That I'm . . ." The words trailed off into a choked silence.

"You're Jennifer Corson." Paul's voice was soft, almost a whisper.

Then Mrs. Hanneman, her voice sounding distant and unreal, spoke: "You took the doll with you to the hospital. You had become so attached to it while— Especially the opals, the eyes. You would look at the eyes for hours, moving the doll around to make them change color. And I let you take it with you. They must have taken it away from you, to put it with the other girl, the one who died. But the eye . . . the doll wasn't made to be played with, and the eye must have come loose, and you . . ."

Her voice trailed off into silence, and Paul repeated, softly: "You're Jennifer Corson." And then: "It was Roslyn Stratton who died twenty years ago."

As Roslyn heard the words—"Roslyn Stratton died!"—she felt weak, and the feeling that had been growing steadily in her stomach suddenly engulfed her entire body.

"Here, sit down," Paul said, half supporting her as he guided her through the door behind the counter and to the battered couch by the workroom window.

Limply, she sat, leaning against the back of the couch and on one arm. Mrs. Hanneman, who had disappeared seconds before, reappeared with a glass of water. She held it out to Roslyn, who took it, shakily, and drank. For a moment she thought it would not stay down, but then the nausea was gone, replaced by a strange numbness.

Paul, she noticed dimly, was seated next to her, one hand still resting on her shoulder. Mrs. Hanneman stood two feet away, still saying nothing, only watching anxiously.

Roslyn looked up at her. "I'm your—your niece?"

The woman nodded stiffly, and Roslyn could see that she wanted nothing more than to throw her arms around Roslyn, but she waited—waited for a signal from Roslyn herself. A signal that

Roslyn knew she could not give, not now, not to this woman—this stranger—standing before her.

"How?" Roslyn heard a strained voice asking, and she realized the voice was her own. "How could something like that have happened? Who could have done it?"

"My father," Paul said flatly, "and Dr. Horace Macklin. We're guessing at a lot, but probably the other baby—the real Roslyn Stratton—died, and my father saw his chance. And he talked Horace into helping him. He must have. He couldn't have done it by himself. Anyway, they made the switch, including the doll. And of course they had to keep Frieda away from the body. Which meant they had to have a closed casket. She would have seen that it wasn't really Jennifer, that it was a different baby. She had kept Jennifer most of the time since her parents had died, and she was the only one who was really close to her."

"But *my* parents—surely *they* would have noticed! How could they help but see the difference? No! It's crazy!"

"I realize it's crazy, but it looks like it's true," Paul insisted quietly. "Remember what you told me? That your parents left Fowler right after you recovered from your illness? That they never returned, not even for a visit? That even today your mother refuses to return? Or to answer questions?"

"You're saying they *knew!*"

"I don't know how *much* they knew. Maybe your mother didn't know about the switch at all. Or maybe she really *did* know, consciously or subconsciously, but she refused to admit it, even to herself. She had thought her baby was dying, and suddenly it was alive and recovering. It was given back to her, almost from the dead. It looked a little different, but that could have been because of the severe illness, and she wasn't about to ask any questions."

He paused for a breath. "It *could* have happened that way. Or a dozen other ways."

"But my father—are you saying *that's* why he moved us so suddenly?"

"I don't know. Maybe he knew, maybe he didn't. But don't forget, the Blassingrames—and my father controlled enough of the estate even then—had a lot of influence. He could have forced your father to sell out. He could have ruined him, one way or another, if he had wanted to. Or he could have simply bought him out at a high price, bribing him to leave, more or less."

"But why would my father accept it? If he knew that I—that their baby had died, and that I was someone else . . ."

Paul shrugged. "The worst way of looking at it is, he did it for the money. The worst way from your viewpoint, at least. Or maybe, even though he knew a mix-up had happened, he didn't know who or why—he might only have known that your mother apparently believed her baby had survived, and he couldn't bring himself to tell her differently. There are a dozen ways it could have happened, a hundred."

Roslyn was silent then, her mind whirling back over the years. All the unanswered questions; the letters from Carl hidden away but not destroyed; her mother's continual apprehension about Fowler; the opal, clutched in her own hand when the fever had suddenly and unexpectedly broken; the repeated dreams about what could only be Jennifer Corson's doll . . .

Yes, she thought, it *is* possible. It's like something out of a nightmare, but it *is* possible.

She looked up at Mrs. Hanneman, then at Paul, still seated beside her, watching her closely.

"What now?" Roslyn asked. Her voice sounded even stranger to her now, flat and emotionless despite the knot that alternately tightened and twisted in her stomach.

Paul shook his head slowly in answer. "I don't know, not yet. But you will have to be very careful not to let on to anyone that you've found out the truth."

"Why? If *you* know—"

"Frankly, I think you could be in danger."

"Danger? But why? From whom?"

"My father knows who you are. That could be enough reason."

"But he wouldn't—"

"He wouldn't?" Paul's laugh was short and harsh. "If you accept the fact of what he and Horace did twenty years ago, you have to accept the strong probability that they will try to protect themselves now." He hesitated. "Who do you think broke into your cottage Monday night?"

A chill ran up her spine, and a vision of Ben Blassingrame, shrouded in darkness, swam before her eyes.

"I see you've got an idea," Paul went on, watching Roslyn's face as it reflected her inner turmoil. "I'll bet it *was* my father, and I'll bet I know what he was looking for. Didn't you say that the intruder acted as if he were searching the top of the bureau? Where you would normally put your ring for the night?"

"Yes . . ."

Paul nodded. "But he couldn't find it."

"I wear it all the time, even in bed," she said softly. Then, blinking: "You *really* think it was him?"

"Him or Horace. And another thing. I'd be willing to bet that your oh-so-convenient virus Saturday night—tell me, did my father —or Horace—give you something to eat or drink after I left you?"

Again there was the shiver as she realized what he was driving at. "Your father," she said, "while you were with Sophie."

"I thought so. Horace has a case full of odds and ends; it wouldn't be any trouble for him to find something that would put you harmlessly out of the way—send you home—for a few hours, just long enough to keep you from meeting Sophie. And to keep Sophie from meeting you, and from seeing you. And your ring."

Again she thought: It's possible. In a world where murder and war are commonplace, *anything* is possible. It could even happen to me . . .

"But he wouldn't harm me, not seriously," she protested. "After all, even if he did give me something in my drink—and I'm not convinced that he did—it only upset my stomach a little. It wasn't anything serious. And it isn't as if he had actually *killed* someone . . ."

"You may be right," Paul said softly. "I hope to hell you are, but I don't think you should take any chances."

"But what can I do? If he knows who I am—"

"Just don't let on to him—to anyone—that *you* know who you are. As long as he thinks you're in the dark, he won't feel compelled to do anything drastic, I'm sure. But if he knew that you had been seeing Frieda . . ."

"But he probably does. Or Dr. Macklin does, at least. I've talked to Eric about it. In fact, I asked him about Jennifer Corson last night. And he asked his father about the name." She paused, remembering what Eric had told her about his father's reaction. "If he was actually involved in the—the switch, that would explain why he was so upset when Eric asked him about the name."

Paul sighed. "And it would explain why *my* father seemed so jumpy this morning. Horace must have told him about it. They must know that you're at least getting close to the truth." He turned to Mrs. Hanneman. "Do they know how much *you* know?"

She shook her head. "I haven't talked to any of them in twenty years," she said, as if that answered the question.

Paul frowned thoughtfully. "They must have guessed by now. But . . . look, *you* could be in danger, too."

"No!" The word exploded from Roslyn. "Not both of us! I just don't believe it! Switching babies is one thing, but murder is something else altogether!"

Paul stood silently for a moment, as if debating with himself. "I know it seems impossible," he said finally, "but you have to remember how much is at stake here."

"I don't care! They're not murderers! Even if what you say is true, they didn't kill anyone. They didn't even *hurt* anyone!"

"Don't forget Jennifer's parents," Paul said, his voice still soft. "The possibility of murder *does* exist there."

Roslyn shook her head, still denying it.

"And your own father," Paul went on, "you said *he* died in an accident, too. When was that? Six years ago?"

She nodded, frowning, apprehensive.

His voice was reluctant as he continued again. "Are you *sure* it was an accident?"

"Of course! What else could it . . ." Her voice trailed off as her mind worked over his question. She felt the knot in her stomach moving, turning colder and tighter as the disintegration of her world continued.

"But they *said* it was an accident! He was driving home from the shop, and the roads were wet . . ." Her voice trailed off as she thought: Another auto accident, like the Corsons . . .

"But how much investigation was there?" Paul was asking. "If no one had any reason to suspect anything but an accident, they wouldn't look very deeply. Any more than they did into the accident that killed Jennifer's parents."

Roslyn shook her head helplessly. "But why? Why would your father or Dr. Macklin want to kill him? Especially then. That was almost fifteen years after—after the switch was made! *If* a switch was made."

"I don't know why." Paul's voice seemed to have grown more calm as Roslyn's had grown more agitated. "As I said, I'm not at all sure that they did kill anyone. I sincerely hope they didn't, but the possibility is there. As for why—" He shrugged. "Was your—was your father having money troubles? Maybe he came back and wanted more money. Maybe he decided he had been taken advantage of the first time. Or maybe it was just the opposite. Maybe his conscience got the better of him and he was threatening to let the truth out. I don't know. Nobody knows. Unless it's my father. Or Horace."

Though Paul's voice remained calm, a new bitterness entered it as he spoke the last half dozen words.

Roslyn, still seated, leaned back on the couch. Strangely, she was beginning to feel numb. It was just too much to accept all at one time. First, she wasn't herself—literally. Then, on top of that was the possibility that her real parents—people she had never seen, people she had never even known existed until yesterday—had been murdered. And now her own father—the man she had known as her father—may also have been murdered.

And, if any of those possibilities was indeed true, there was the additional possibility that she herself was in danger.

Suddenly, she felt like running, but she didn't know where to run to. She didn't know *who* to run to. It was like a nightmare, where everything shifted from second to second, where there were no rules and no reasons. With her world so totally altered, who was there that she could still trust? Her mother? But there was a good possibility that her mother *wasn't* her mother at all . . .

She looked up at Paul and Mrs. Hanneman—her aunt? The older woman was standing silently, her face a mask. Paul's expression was grim, but concern seemed to fill his eyes.

"But you, of all people—" Roslyn blurted. "How did *you* find out?"

"*I* didn't. All I did was remember—finally—where I had heard the name of Jennifer Corson. The Corsons had lived in that cottage that you're living in now—"

"But if they were Blassingrames—"

"Why didn't they live in the 'mansion'? I have no idea. As I recall —I was only six or seven at the time—Aunt Sophie and Ruth lived alone, except for the servants. When Ruth married Corson, she moved into the cottage. Maybe for just a honeymoon, I don't know. But apparently they stayed there, and Sophie stayed alone in the mansion. It wasn't until ten years ago that my father and I moved into the mansion with Sophie. Once Father started taking over all the business operations—or when Sophie finally decided to turn them over to him—I guess they wanted to make it official." Paul shrugged. "I never have understood all these family and business things. But I guess this lack of business understanding runs in our branch of the family—except for my father, of course. Except for Benjamin Blassingrame II. Ben Number One inherited just as much as Sophie's husband did, but he didn't do nearly as well. Oh, he didn't go broke, or anything like that, but compared to what Sophie did with her half—or her husband's half, I should say—it was the same as going broke."

He stopped, shaking his head. "But that's a sidetrack. As I started to say, *I* didn't find out anything at all. I just remembered who the Corsons were, and I came here to see Frieda. She already had a pretty good idea of what had happened. Once she saw you— and the ring—she spotted the resemblances almost immediately, the same as Horace and my father did. And when you told her about your being in the hospital at about the right time twenty years ago —well, together with everything that had happened when Jennifer supposedly died, it wasn't hard for her to guess the truth. So, when I came to see her this morning, just after I talked to you on the phone, it all came out. Just like it probably would have come out tonight, or whenever *you* saw her next."

He looked toward the older woman questioningly. "Am I right?"

Mrs. Hanneman nodded, but her eyes were still on Roslyn. "You're the image of your mother."

The words, simply, softly spoken, jolted Roslyn as much as anything had so far. Her mother . . .

No, no matter what the "truth" was, the word "mother" only brought forth one image, and it was not the image of a woman who had died twenty years before, whose likeness lived on only in a doll —and in herself.

Roslyn swallowed audibly, took a deep breath in an effort to calm herself. She looked again toward Paul.

"What now? What can we do?"

He shook his head slowly back and forth. "Right now, I don't know. This is as sudden for me as it is for you. And if you think it's a shock to discover that your parents aren't really your parents, it's not much better to discover that your father may be a murderer. No, I don't know what we should do—except be very careful not to let out even a hint that you know the truth. Maybe there's some way we can *prove* who you are, and then . . . Look, I've got a couple of ideas, and a few things I can check on today. Maybe tonight we'll be able to come up with something practical. Why don't you go back to the library now, and try to go about your business normally, if that's possible, and come back here tonight, say about eight. Maybe I'll have found something worthwhile by then." He shrugged again. "Unless you have a better idea? Either of you?"

Roslyn started to shake her head, an automatic motion, but she stopped. "What about Sophie? Maybe we should tell her. If my resemblance to her daughter is as strong as you say . . ."

Paul thought for a moment. "It's a possibility. But don't forget, they prevented you from seeing her Saturday at the party. And now that they're on their guard . . ."

He was silent another moment, frowning thoughtfully. "But it's a possibility," he went on. "In fact, we'll have to see her eventually, no matter what we do now. But we'll have to be careful—and not only because of Horace and my father. Don't forget, she's in her eighties. And if we suddenly confront her with a granddaughter she thought was dead for twenty years, especially a granddaughter who looks so much like her daughter . . . not to mention all the rest. It's been pretty much of a shock to me, and I'm barely a third of her age."

"I understand," Roslyn said, feeling once again the shock that had overwhelmed her when she had first realized that it all might be true. "But what about other relatives? There must be others who would remember my—who would remember Ruth Corson and would see the resemblance."

"I'm sure there are. But would they believe it's anything but a coincidence? They might even think it was all a plot. They might figure you were a phony who had somehow learned about what happened twenty years ago, and . . . well, you know how it works. But you're right. That's something else I can do this afternoon—sound out a few of the other Blassingrames. Maybe by tonight, we'll have a better idea of where we stand."

He laughed abruptly. "Where *we* stand! You know, I just realized what I'm doing. I'm cutting my own throat, that's what I'm doing. If we prove you're really Jennifer Corson, that means my father is very likely out in the cold, if not in jail, especially if it turns out that he and Horace had something to do with any of those deaths. And if *he* is out, so am I."

Roslyn frowned. "But your aunt couldn't blame *you* for what your father did twenty years ago."

He shrugged. "Not logically, I suppose, but who said that Sophie was logical? In the first place, I don't think she's ever been too thrilled about me anyway. Besides, if my father doesn't inherit a lot of stuff, then I don't either." A grin crossed his face. "Unless you want to share it, of course. If all this is true, then you're about my second—or maybe third—cousin, which isn't really *too* close a relationship . . ."

He reached down and took her hand, pulling her to her feet. "But right now, you had better get back to the library." He laughed, but there was a seriousness in his voice. "Just try to act natural, especially if my father or Horace—or Sheriff Eric—shows up."

He squeezed her hands, and for a moment he seemed about to lean over and plant a quick kiss on her face, but he didn't. Instead, he looked at her silently for a moment, then said: "You're quite a girl, Roslyn—or Jennifer, I suppose it should be—dedication and all. You know, you haven't once asked the obvious question."

"What obvious question? I've asked so many. And gotten such rotten answers."

He laughed suddenly. "Obvious to me, maybe not to you. How much is it all worth? How much will you eventually inherit?"

Again, just as she thought she had fully recovered from the series of "revelations," she was shaken by his words. Of course! she thought, the Blassingrame estate . . .

She shook her head, trying to force the thoughts out of her mind. She didn't even want to think about it, not now, not till the other things were settled. Learning that she was another person was bad enough, but now, realizing that that other person would very likely be rich in the not too distant future . . .

Again she shook her head, more violently this time. "No, don't even tell me about it. Let me get used to the rest of this first." A lopsided smile pulled at her lips, a smile that was more defense than amusement. "If I survive long enough to get used to it, that is."

"Don't worry," Paul said, with another squeeze of her hands, "you'll survive. I'll see to it."

"That's a guarantee?"

"A guarantee, a personal guarantee. I got you into all this, it's the least I can do to see you through." He stopped, and a bleakness seemed to cloud his face briefly. "And it may be one of the very few worthwhile things I've done in—"

Again he stopped short, and his near-professional smile reappeared. "In any event, as long as we keep quiet about this, we're all safe." He looked more closely at her. "You *didn't* tell Eric anything at lunch, did you? After I left?"

She laughed herself. "No, my compulsive honesty didn't quite trip me up. Almost, but not quite."

"Good. Now this evening, it might be a good idea for you to have supper at your cousin's house. Just to be absolutely safe. Didn't you tell me you were planning to go there this evening anyway?"

"But you said I'd be safe until—"

"Nothing is certain, not now. And don't forget, there's already been one 'burglary' at your cottage. No one would be overly surprised at a second, more violent one."

Abruptly, as if it had been pulled by a huge elastic band, her mind snapped back to Monday night, and the shadowy form of the intruder swam before her eyes. And once again she thought: Yes, it is possible. *It really is possible!*

"All right," she said, "but this can't go on very long. I don't think I can take it, whether any of it is true or not."

"Don't worry," he assured her. "I think we'll be ready after tonight. Just give me a chance to check a couple of things, and—" He stopped, looking at both of the women. "And if it doesn't work out the way I hope, we'll go directly to Sophie. If we work up to it the right way, it will be all right. She's a pretty tough old bird, even if she is almost ninety. And I'll just come right out and tell my father that I know the truth. He won't dare do anything then. He knows damned well I'd blow the whistle on him!" He laughed harshly. "As you may have noticed at the party, we do not see precisely eye to eye on a number of things, so he knows I wouldn't hesitate a second if anything happened to you—or to you," he added, turning toward Mrs. Hanneman.

He took a deep breath and seemed to relax. "Yes, I think everything will be okay by this evening. Everything will be worked out, one way or another."

CHAPTER 18

Vivian came to the door when Roslyn knocked.

"Roslyn! How are you? I just today heard what happened—your burglary! I didn't see it in the paper last night, and someone at the office today—"

"I'm fine," Roslyn reassured her, but couldn't help adding to herself: So far.

Once she had returned to the library, only a few minutes late after all, she had thrown herself into her work in an attempt to keep her mind off what she had just learned, but it hadn't worked that way. A half hour of attempting to read—and understand—the reviews in last week's New York *Times Book Review* proved only that she couldn't concentrate on anything longer than two sentences. Going over the last week's circulation and use statistics proved a little easier, but trying to incorporate them into the quarterly report to the library board was another matter. Even inserting cards for new books into the card file proved to be more than she could cope with efficiently, and after going back to check what she had already done and finding at least a half dozen cards misfiled, she gave up on anything that required the least bit of concentration. In the end, she had sorted through the last month's accumulation of "discard or rebind," and that had proved to be about the right level of mental activity. It didn't take a great deal of concentration to decide that a book with the cover torn half off but otherwise intact could be rebound while one that had several pages glued together with chocolate syrup had to be discarded. Even in that and the equally mechanical and repetitive task of making out book order slips, though, she found herself staring blankly into space every few minutes. A half dozen times, she had started toward the telephone, and once she had even gotten as far as looking up the Blassingrame number, but when it came down to it, she had not been able to follow through. She had not been able to telephone Ben Blassingrame and tell him that she had learned "the truth," and that Paul knew it as well. Whether she was afraid of what he would do or was simply afraid of sounding like an utter fool, she wasn't sure. Probably it was a bit of both because, back in the sane and everyday surroundings of the library, the very idea that she was not really Roslyn Stratton seemed insane. But each time she decided it was all nonsense, she would come across a book order for one of their ever popular true-crime books, and she would be back to believing that, at the very least, it was possible.

Another half dozen times, she had decided to call her mother at the store where she worked, but the decision never lasted until she could reach a telephone. Even if this insanity did turn out to be true, she would have to be face to face with her mother when she told her. If it was really true, and if it was this very thing which had caused her mother's odd behavior toward Fowler all these years, then a simple telephone call would be useless.

"Hi, Mom, I don't want to make you feel bad, but you're not really my mother." She could just imagine herself saying something like that over the phone. It would be difficult enough to explain in person.

So, in the end, she had followed Paul's advice, however unintentionally, and had talked to no one about it—except Grommet, who had again deserted his window and had insisted on stalking back and forth across Roslyn's book order slips, including the ones she was still trying to make out.

And now, as she followed Vivian toward the kitchen, she could only wish that the day were already over—or that it had never happened to begin with. But as she looked down at Vivian, she couldn't help but think: I should always have suspected that something was odd. I'm like a square peg in a family of round holes. I don't look like my mother *or* my father, and certainly not like Carl or Vivian. Taller than any of them, even the men, and a totally different bone structure . . .

"But a burglar!" Vivian was saying, as they entered the kitchen and Vivian motioned for Roslyn to sit down on one of the chairs near the table. "You could have been killed!"

"I doubt it," Roslyn said, lowering herself onto the chair. "Burglars aren't normally violent. Or so everyone tells me."

"But what happened? The paper didn't say much." Vivian kept her eyes on Roslyn as she resumed putting the finishing touches on a casserole and slipped it into the oven.

"Not much of anything happened," Roslyn said. She would sooner not have talked about it at all, she told herself, but she went on to describe the whole episode anyway, being careful to avoid any hints about the identity of the intruder.

Vivian shuddered when Roslyn had finished. "I don't care what you say. I would have been petrified."

"I wasn't particularly calm," Roslyn said, and for a moment she was tempted to continue, to tell Vivian the whole thing.

But she didn't. Even as she framed the opening sentences in her mind, it sounded more ridiculous than ever.

After an awkward silence, Vivian looked hopefully at Roslyn. "Can you stay for supper?"

"If you're sure it's not too much trouble."

"Of course not." A broad smile spread across Vivian's rounded face. And then: "Would you want to stay here overnight? After the break-in, I thought you might not want to be alone at the cottage."

Roslyn shook her head. "Thanks, but I'm sure I'll be all right. I doubt that anything will happen."

Another silence, and then Roslyn asked: "Have you seen Tom Lory since Saturday? You two seemed to hit it off pretty well."

Vivian nodded. "He stopped in at the office today." She smiled, a little embarrassedly. "Mr. Hardigan, my boss, was teasing me all afternoon."

"How about your father? Does he object?"

Vivian shook her head. "He hasn't said anything yet, except what you heard Sunday. But he doesn't know I have a date with him tonight."

Roslyn frowned, looking at the oven. "A date? *After* supper?"

"I couldn't very well go before. Father expects—"

"Damn it, Viv!" Roslyn exploded, startled at her own vehemence. "Can't he get his own supper—or eat out, even—just once? How long can you—"

Roslyn stopped, and suddenly she wondered: If all this *does* turn out to be true, and I am a wealthy heiress, the first thing I'll do is—

But what *could* she do for Vivian? What could money alone do for her? Money wasn't the problem here. The problem was that she was totally dominated by her father, and she always would be.

"Viv," Roslyn said, her anger under control again, "did Tom Lory ask you to go to dinner with him?"

"Yes, but—"

"But nothing! You get on that phone and call him and tell him he can pick you up as soon as he's ready."

"But the supper—"

"You've got it half made already. You just get on that phone, and —you tell him to meet you somewhere away from here, somewhere in town. That will avoid any scenes with your father."

And Roslyn wondered: Is this really me? There was a feeling of unreality, as if she were watching and listening to a total stranger angrily issuing orders, easily taking charge. Was this what the mere prospect of money did to her? But she continued, answering another of Vivian's protests with a peremptory wave of her hand.

"Don't worry about your father. I'll take care of him this evening. Now you get on that phone, or I'm going to make the call myself. And then if I have to, I'll drag you out to the car and drive you into town myself."

Still Vivian hesitated, and Roslyn turned and went to the telephone alcove. "Well, what's his number? Or do I have to look it up myself?"

"Five-eight-three-two-four."

Roslyn smiled faintly and dialed. On the second ring, a man's voice answered. "Lory."

"Tom Lory? This is Roslyn Stratton. I'm just calling to let you know that my cousin—Vivian—can have dinner with you after all."

"Wonderful! How soon shall I—"

"She'll meet you at—at the northwest corner of the courthouse square in ten minutes."

"All right, but why—"

"Ten minutes," Roslyn repeated, and hung up. She turned to Vivian, who was still standing in the kitchen, her mouth partially open. "Now come on, get rid of that apron and get moving. You don't want to keep him waiting."

When Vivian still did nothing, Roslyn hurried around behind her and loosened the apron. "What's the matter? Don't you *want* to have supper with him?"

"Yes, but—"

"No more buts! Get moving. I told you, I'll take care of your father."

Then, slowly at first but with gathering speed, Vivian began to move.

"Come on," Roslyn said five minutes later, "I'll drive you to town myself, just to make sure you don't change your mind halfway there."

Taking Vivian's arm, Roslyn kept her going until they were both in Roslyn's ancient Rambler. Within another five minutes, they were waiting at the corner of the courthouse square. Vivian was still overwhelmed by the sudden rush of activity and a little worried about her father's reaction, but it was obvious that Vivian was, underneath it all, glad that it had happened. Tom Lory was only a couple of minutes late, and Roslyn waved to them both as they drove away.

Roslyn drove back to the house at a leisurely pace. Strangely, she felt relaxed for the first time since noon. The sudden explosion of activity, purposeful and satisfying—and surprising!—seemed to have calmed her, almost driven the other thoughts from her mind.

As she pulled into the driveway, she saw that Carl's car was back. Well, she thought, trying to recapture the feeling of recklessness that had gripped her only minutes before, this is it. I said I'd handle Carl, and here's my chance. At least it will give me something to do until eight o'clock.

Carl appeared at the back door even before Roslyn was out of the car.

"Where is Vivian?" His voice, almost a shout, was high pitched, shrill.

Roslyn was startled at the intensity of the voice. She had expected annoyance, even anger, but Carl's voice seemed on the verge of panic. And then she remembered the tone that had been in his voice Sunday. "She's all I have left!" he had said then, and hidden beneath the anger, had been the same fear that had now completely surfaced.

"She has a date tonight," Roslyn said, as she approached Carl. "Tom Lory is taking her out to dinner and a movie."

Carl stood blocking the door, and Roslyn wasn't sure that he had understood her words. "She'll be back in a few hours," she went on. Strangely, despite what she had felt before, she couldn't help but feel a tinge of sympathy—no, sympathy was the wrong word. It was pity, not sympathy.

"Supper is in the oven," she said. "If you don't mind my staying, I'll finish it and fix the rest."

Slowly, he stood back, allowing her to pass. He stood watching as she moved about the kitchen, getting the rest of the meal together.

"She didn't tell me," he said finally, the fear in his voice now converted largely into irritation.

Roslyn glanced toward him as she continued opening a package of frozen vegetables.

"She was afraid to," Roslyn said flatly. "She was going to fix supper here and *then* go out with him. But I made her go ahead."

"You? But why? If she didn't want to—"

Roslyn crumpled the empty vegetable package angrily and threw it into a wastebasket. "But she *did* want to! That's the point! Can't you see? She did want to go, but she was afraid of what you would say!"

"But she knows she can do whatever she wants!"

"She does?"

He blinked, as if unable to comprehend Roslyn's question. "Of course."

"Then why was she afraid to tell you about it? It's not as if she were running away to get married—though I wouldn't blame her if she did, one of these days."

Carl Jefferson shook his head, his face still not registering comprehension. "I don't believe it, I just don't believe it." The irritation was once more blending into uncertainty, even fear. "You forced her, you said so yourself. You said—"

Abruptly he stopped. His head continued to move from side to side as if it were an automatic action not under his conscious control, and then he hurried through the kitchen toward the living room. She heard the click of the TV set being turned on, and a second later, the faint creaking of the overstuffed chair as he sat down.

Only in his middle fifties, she thought, and already he's an old man. Despite herself, she still felt a certain pity for him. For whatever reason, he had not been able to adjust to his life. His sister had left him without so much as telling him, or ever writing to him afterward. His wife had died and except for Vivian he had been alone.

But both of those had been years ago. There was no reason for him to continue this way, no reason at all—no more reason than there was for her mother to continue to avoid Fowler so completely . . .

And with that thought, another tremor ran up her spine. Maybe there *was* a reason. Maybe there was even more to it than what Paul had told her that afternoon. Maybe . . .

But no, no matter what the reasons, Carl's actions with Vivian were inexcusable. They were hurting Vivian; they *had* hurt her, until now, at the age of nearly thirty, she was afraid even to tell her father about a date she had for the evening. No, there was no excuse.

But even so, as she remembered the panicky edge to Carl's voice as he had stood waiting at the back door, she could not entirely uproot that lingering tinge of pity.

Supper was eaten mostly in silence. Though Carl seemed to have recovered his composure, there was still an air of nervousness just below the surface, as if he had been deprived of an invisible security blanket. Which, Roslyn thought, as the meal neared completion, was not too far from the truth. At the slightest sound, Carl would look up from the table, and every car that passed on the road outside drew his eyes toward the front of the house and it seemed to be an effort for him not to go to the window and look out.

And she thought: I should have arranged to be here when Vivian gets back.

Eventually supper was over, and without a word, Carl retreated once again into the living room. A few seconds later, the muted sound of the TV set reached her ears. Another security blanket, she thought, as she began to clear the table.

The telephone rang as she put the last of the dishes from the drying rack into the cabinets above the sink. She glanced toward the alcove, and when there was no indication that Carl was coming from the living room, she crossed the kitchen and picked up the receiver.

She half expected to hear Vivian's voice, calling to reassure her father that she would indeed be back this evening, but it was Eric Macklin instead.

"I wondered if you'd be out there," he said. "I tried the cottage and there was no answer."

"I'm just taking Vivian's place for the evening," she said, not explaining further.

There was only a brief hesitation to indicate that Eric had heard her. "You remember that name you mentioned to me? Jennifer Corson?"

Suddenly, Roslyn was back from limbo. All of the afternoon's memories, which she had managed to force to the back of her mind for a few minutes, surged forward again.

"I remember," she said, and she wondered if her voice sounded as shaky as she felt. "Did you find out anything?"

"I found out she would have been a very rich girl if she had lived. Her mother's maiden name was Blassingrame. The woman was Sophie Blassingrame's daughter."

"How did you— Did your father finally admit that he knew the name after all?"

"My father? No, I haven't even talked to him this afternoon— although I think I'll tackle him now that I know who Jennifer Corson was. Maybe it will refresh his memory. No, the way I found out was simple enough. You told me she died about twenty years ago, so I looked up the newspaper files at the *Journal* office. It wasn't hard to find. Jennifer made the front pages, not just the obituary section. And it told all about her family connections, of course. 'The last direct descendant of matriarch Sophie Blassingrame.'"

Roslyn was silent, not sure how to go on. She didn't dare ask him the question that was on her mind: Was there any evidence of foul play? Not only could it be risky, but it also sounded dumb, she realized. If there had been any evidence, there would have been an investigation, and there hadn't been.

"Anything else?" she asked finally.

"Are you all right, Ros?" Eric's voice came back a second later.

"Of course. Why shouldn't I be?"

"I don't know. Your voice sounded a little odd, that's all."

She forced a small laugh. "I just went through a small trauma with Vivian," she said, and went on to explain briefly what had happened.

"Good for you," Eric said. "I saw Tom yesterday, and unless I miss my guess, he's very much taken with your cousin. And if anyone can stand up to Carl Jefferson, he can."

"I hope so, but I'm afraid they may be in for a scene when he brings her home tonight." She lowered her voice as she spoke, glancing toward the living room and listening to the voices from the TV set for a moment.

"It'll be all right," Eric assured her. "Tom can take care of himself—and your cousin, too." He paused briefly. "Look, Ros, are you sure you're all right? You still sound a little odd."

Again she forced a small laugh. "Is that what comes of being a sheriff? You become suspicious of everyone?"

"No, just people who suddenly start sounding odd when they talk to me."

And Roslyn wondered: Should she tell him? Should she meet him somewhere and tell him? Surely *he* couldn't be in on any plot, any more than Paul could. He was even younger than Paul, not more than five or six when Jennifer and her parents had died.

And she wanted to tell *someone!* Now that the furore with Vivian was at least temporarily over and she had nothing to do but wait, all the nervousness that had afflicted her throughout the afternoon was returning with a vengeance. And unless she told someone—or went in and got into a fight with Carl—there was nothing she could do but wait.

She glanced at her watch, and she realized that there wasn't as much time as she had thought. Barely a half hour. But still . . .

"Tell me," she said finally, "what sort of a man is Benjamin Blassingrame?"

"What kind of man? Besides rich, you mean?"

"Yes, besides rich. Is there even the slightest possibility that he could hurt someone? Seriously hurt them, I mean?"

"You mean physically?" His voice sounded puzzled. "Or financially?"

"Physically. Could he?"

He seemed to consider it a moment. "I don't know. If he got angry enough, maybe. But almost anyone can do that if he's angry enough."

"I don't mean when he's angry. I mean, could he harm someone in cold blood? Without anger?"

"I doubt it. But why are you asking something like that?"

Why, indeed? "No reason," she started to say, but she stopped as she realized it would sound as foolish to Eric as it did to her. She shouldn't have asked the question about Ben in the first place. For one thing, it was a stupid question, and for another, she hadn't really expected a worthwhile answer.

But she *had* asked it, and now she was stuck with it. And maybe, she thought, that was the real reason, to get herself stuck with it.

Her subconscious was pulling tricks on her again, maybe. She had wanted to tell someone, so her subconscious had blurted out the question about Ben Blassingrame, neatly trapping her into a situation in which she would have no choice but to go further.

"It's a long story," she said finally. "Can you meet me at Mrs. Hanneman's shop?"

"Tonight?" He sounded surprised.

"Yes, tonight." She glanced at her watch again. Seven thirty-five. "Make it a half hour," she said, "eight o'clock."

"All right." The inflection showed that the surprise had yielded to puzzlement.

And she thought: I should warn him not to tell his father, but that would be the quickest way to get him to do just that.

"Eight o'clock," she repeated, and as she hung up she wondered if, this time, her subconscious hadn't gone a little too far.

CHAPTER 19

The sun had been down at least a half hour when Roslyn walked out the back door of the Jefferson house, and the last traces of twilight were disappearing. A cool wind had sprung up out of the north, and she felt the gooseflesh prickling at her arms as she hurried toward the Rambler. The door opened with the usual grating sound and she reached in, picking up the light blue jacket from where she had left it draped across the back of the seat.

Shrugging into the jacket, she slid into the car and coaxed the engine into life. As she backed onto the road and the headlights swung across the ditch and centered themselves on the uneven blacktop surface, leaving the yard in darkness, the thought pushed its way into her mind: When I return here, what will it be like? Will I still be Roslyn Stratton? Or will this whole thing have turned out to be nonsense? Or . . . ?

Melodrama! she told herself sharply. Pure melodrama! But somehow she couldn't quite push the thoughts out of her mind, not completely. The darkness around her, with only a few stars in an almost cloudless sky, seemed to make it all seem more real, more possible.

And she thought of Paul, who seemed even more inclined to make it into a melodrama than she did, with his suspicions of murder and danger and secrecy. Well, she had already blown the secrecy, and there was nothing that could be done about that. Eric would be there, whether Paul wanted him to be or not. Although, she thought, I probably should at least try to warn Paul.

At the corner of Twelfth and Main, next to the Heyde service station, she spotted a phone booth, and on an impulse pulled in. While the young man—with the name "Jim" sewed on the front of his gray uniform—filled the car with gas and did other arcane things under the hood, Roslyn went to the phone booth and dialed the Blassingrames' number.

A male voice answered.

"Is Paul there?" she asked, not sure if it was Paul who had answered or not.

"Miss Stratton?"

Startled that her voice had been recognized, she answered an automatic "Yes."

"This is Ben Blassingrame, Miss Stratton." He sounded as if he were making an effort to keep his voice casual, but the effort was not totally successful. "I meant to inquire yesterday, but I never quite got around to it. How are you feeling now?"

"Just fine. Dr. Macklin gave me a clean bill of health."

"That's good, very good. And how are things going at the library?"

"Just fine," she repeated.

"You feel that you're going to like it here in Fowler, then?"

"I think so. Everything seems very nice so far."

"Paul said that you were a little troubled yesterday. He thought you might even be considering going back to—where was it? Wisconsin?"

"Yes, Wisconsin, but I'm not thinking of leaving. Not right now, at least."

A hesitation. "Good, good. Glad to hear it. I was afraid you might have let that little incident the other night put you off."

"The break-in? No, not at all. I can't imagine that whoever did it will be back. It was probably just a mistake in the first place."

Another pause before Blassingrame replied. "Yes, I suppose it must have been. The cottage had been empty for so long . . . But you said you wanted to talk to Paul?"

"That's right. Is he there?"

"I think so. He was here for dinner, anyway. But what was it you wanted to talk to him about?"

"Nothing important," she said, and she wondered if her voice was betraying her, as it had with Eric.

"If there's anything *I* can do for you . . . ?"

"No, I don't think so."

"I see." Another hesitation, longer this time. "Let me see if he's still here."

There was the clack of the receiver being laid down, and then silence. As she waited, she looked again at her watch. Fifteen to eight. Even if Paul had been there when she had first called, he could have left by now.

Eventually, Blassingrame's voice returned. "I'm afraid you missed him, Miss Stratton. I think he just left."

"That's all right," she said, and then, almost automatically, added, "I'll be seeing him in a few minutes anyway."

Now why, she wondered, even before she had finished the sentence, had she added that? Her nerves, she suspected, making her rattle on when she would be better off not saying anything. Or that damned subconscious again?

"Oh?" Blassingrame's voice had developed a sudden concern. "Where will you be seeing him?"

"At the— In town." Her voice, she knew, even as the words came out, was again sounding "odd."

"I see," he said, after a brief silence. "Incidentally, Paul tells me you were asking about someone—Jennifer Corson, I think he said."

Again? Roslyn thought, but she said: "That's right. I understand she was a relative of Frieda Hanneman."

"Frieda Hanneman?"

"Yes, Frieda Hanneman," Roslyn said, and she had the feeling she and Blassingrame were playing a game, fencing, jockeying for position. "The woman who owns the gift shop south of town."

"Oh yes, I remember seeing it occasionally. I just didn't recognize the name."

I'll bet, she thought, but she said: "What about Jennifer Corson? Did you recognize *that* name?"

There was a longer pause this time. "It sounds familiar, but . . . I'm afraid I can't place it right now. Is it important?"

"No, I suppose not," she said, but she knew that her voice was still betraying her, game or no game. "It was just someone that Frieda Hanneman mentioned, someone who died a long time ago."

"I see." Still another hesitation, even longer, and Roslyn wondered why she didn't simply hang up. Then, abruptly: "Did it have anything to do with your ring?"

Suddenly the game was serious. Paul was right, she thought, and the sudden reality of it twisted at her stomach. "My ring?" was all she could think of to say.

"Yes, the opal ring. The one you were wearing at the party Saturday night."

"I'm surprised that you remembered," she forced herself to say, "but I don't see how—"

"It does have something to do with the ring, then." There was a resigned, dull tone to his voice now, and she knew that her own voice had, as usual, let her down.

"I don't understand," she began, still trying, but he cut her off, his voice still flat.

"I don't suppose you do understand," he said, "not completely. Just how much *do* you know?"

"About what?" Still she kept up the pretense, uselessly.

Blassingrame was silent then for several seconds. Finally she could hear him suck in his breath before he spoke.

"All right, Miss Stratton," he said, "it's about time it was over. Horace was right. He's always been right."

"Dr. Macklin? What does he—"

"There's no need to pretend, Miss Stratton, no need at all." The tiredness in his voice seemed suddenly overwhelming. "Come to the house and we'll get everything straightened out. As much as is possible after all this time."

"*Your* house, you mean? When?"

"Yes, our house. Sophie's house. The sooner, the better."

And Roslyn thought: Why not? This is what we were planning to do anyway, eventually. But she should still talk to Paul first.

"Tonight?" she asked. "Or tomorrow?"

"Tonight. I don't think— Yes, tonight."

She hesitated. If she met Paul—and Eric—at Mrs. Hanneman's, and if they all three went to Blassingrame's, they would certainly be safe, even if Paul's wildest speculations were true. After all, Paul had said that, if worse came to worse, he would simply let his father know that he had found out the truth. And a meeting with Ben Blassingrame was what it would all come down to in the end anyway, either now or the next day or the next week. It might as well be gotten out of the way immediately, especially since Roslyn had, so to speak, let the cat out of the bag.

"All right," she said finally. "Give me a half hour."

"I would suggest you not wait to meet Paul, wherever it was you planned to meet him," he said. "Come directly here."

"All right," Roslyn lied, and for once she managed to stop without blurting out anything else.

She couldn't be sure, but she thought she could detect a note of relief in Blassingrame's voice as he told her he would be waiting for her to arrive.

She returned to the car, where the gray-uniformed Jim stood waiting. "It needed a quart of oil, too, lady. That'll be eight fifty-seven altogether."

As he counted out the change from the metal change holder around his waist, he added, "It could use a tune-up, too, but we don't do that sort of thing around here."

"Don't worry about it," she said, holding in a sudden impulse to laugh, "maybe I'll buy a new one next week."

Jim looked at her blankly, then at the car. He nodded then, and as the engine reluctantly revived itself, said, "Yeah, lady, that's a good idea. Better than a tune-up any day."

Five minutes later she pulled to a stop at Mrs. Hanneman's shop. No other car was in the gravel parking area at the side, and the front of the shop was dark. A dim light was visible through the window to the workroom, though, and Roslyn walked around to the back and up the half dozen steps to the narrow wooden porch.

Mrs. Hanneman, when she came to the door, was wearing a pair of faded jeans and a paint-spotted man's shirt. Her short, graying hair, normally carefully arranged in bangs, was disheveled, as if she had been running her fingers through it repeatedly. She was, Roslyn thought, a totally different woman from the one she had been during any of the other visits.

Mrs. Hanneman smiled when she saw Roslyn, and the dim light from the room behind her seemed to soften the lines of her face. Indicating her clothes, she said, "I've been doing some modeling, just something to keep myself busy."

"I know how you feel," Roslyn said, looking around the room. "I haven't been able to concentrate on much of anything myself this afternoon."

The overhead fluorescent lights were off, and the only illumination was from a small fluorescent drafting lamp clamped to one edge of the huge work table in the middle of the room. The shelves and cabinets and pegboards around the walls were half hidden in shadow, and the one glass-fronted cabinet filled with piles of tiny arms and legs and torsos and heads looked vaguely macabre.

A half dozen skeletal bodies, apparently made from bent and twisted coat hangers, lay on the table under the light. Several pairs of nylon stockings and pantyhose lay near the bodies. Mrs. Hanneman returned to the table and picked up one of the pantyhose, one leg of which was already spiral-cut into a single, narrow strip.

"This is always a good time killer," she said, taking up a pair of scissors and beginning to work on the second leg. "I wrap those wire skeletons with the strips of nylon. I have another pair of scissors if you'd like to cut a few strips yourself. I can always use the spare bodies."

Roslyn looked around again. On the far end of the table, on its small metal stand, was the portable electric kiln. The door and peephole were both closed and the tiny red light on the front indicated it was turned on.

"More ceramics?" Roslyn asked.

The older woman looked up from her cutting. "A head," she said. "The first firing should be finished in an hour or so."

"A doll's head?"

Mrs. Hanneman nodded, lowering her eyes. Some of the reserve Roslyn had seen in her before seemed to return. "I'm not sure what it will be. I may—"

Then Roslyn's eyes fell on something that lay almost in the shadow of the kiln, near the back edge of the table. The book of doll photos, its red cover almost black in the shadows. She looked back toward Mrs. Hanneman then, and the woman's eyes met Roslyn's and seemed to reach out to her for a moment.

Mrs. Hanneman blinked and shook her head lightly, forcing a faint smile. "It may seem foolish to you, but . . ." Her eyes lowered, and she began cutting the pantyhose again. "It won't be nearly as good as the original, of course, the one my mother made. I've never been as good as she was. And this one is clay, not wax. To make a wax one, I'd have to make a mold first, and I haven't done much in wax since— But I want you to have it when I'm done, no matter how these other things turn out. I don't have opals for the eyes, of course . . ."

A chill shot through Roslyn at the thought of the doll head baking in the kiln, a duplicate of the one that now lay in the grave with—

With Roslyn Stratton?

The magic of a name, she thought, shuddering. She started to refuse the doll the woman was making, but then she thought: Don't be foolish. Don't hurt her feelings. She's just trying to do a little sympathetic magic, that's all. Whether I'm Jennifer or not, she *wants* me to be Jennifer, so she's going to make me a doll like the one her mother had given to Jennifer twenty years ago. Just a little subconscious sympathetic magic, that's all. Harmless and a little sad. Even if Roslyn did turn out to be, physically, Jennifer Corson, it would not make a lot of difference. The person that Jennifer would have become—the girl who would have been Frieda Hanneman's niece—*was* dead. She could never be resurrected, no matter what happened now. The name could be brought back to life and applied to a totally different person, but that was all.

"Thank you," Roslyn said simply. "That's very nice of you." She moved toward the end of the table that held the kiln. She could feel the heat radiating from it.

"You said it would take another hour? How hot does it have to get?"

Frieda Hanneman thought for a second, looking up from her cutting. "It's a cone oh-five," she said. "I think that's around nineteen hundred degrees."

Roslyn pursed her lips in a silent whistle. "That's hot." She held her hand out toward the kiln. "No wonder it's giving off so much heat. Is it safe to have it sitting on the table that way?"

"A small one like that is all right. It's designed for table-top use. And, for a kiln, it's pretty portable. When I talk to the craft classes in high school, this is what I take with me. I can't quite carry it by myself, but there's always a student who's more than willing to take the time off from his other classes to help."

"I'm sure," Roslyn said. "But that heat—you don't actually fire it up in the demonstrations, do you?"

"No, it would take too long to get heated up, and just as long to cool off so it could be moved. Some of the kids do come out here to look at it in action, though. They're usually disappointed, though. There isn't that much to see, especially through the peephole. If you look at just the right time, you can see the cones melting, but that's about all. The thing the kids are usually most impressed with at first is the temperature, especially when I tell them that it gets more than twice as hot in there as your self-cleaning ovens do. And more than four times as hot as the hottest normal setting of an oven. And you'd be surprised—or maybe you wouldn't—at how many of them want to put something inside, just to see what happens. They usually lose interest when they find out it takes at least three hours to get up to temperature."

"Do you have to stay with it the whole time? Or can you leave it? I was looking at what few books we have on ceramics at the library—in case that program I was thinking about ever actually happens—and one of them said that some kilns have—I think they called them 'kiln sitters.'"

Mrs. Hanneman nodded. "Yes, I have this one hooked up so that it goes off automatically when the cone melts, but I hate to leave it alone until it's cooled down."

"But you could if you had to?"

"Yes, but I still—why do you ask?"

"We're supposed to go to see Ben Blassingrame in a few minutes."

"Ben? But I thought we weren't doing anything until we talked with Paul."

"We're not. But as soon as Paul gets here—and the sheriff—we're all going to see Ben."

"Why? What happened?"

"I don't know for sure, but I talked to Ben on the phone a few minutes ago, and he already knows about us."

"But how?" A mixture of puzzlement and fear had begun to show in the older woman's face.

"It's partly my fault, I'm afraid," Roslyn said, "but I think he was already fairly sure even before I talked to him. Paul had asked him about Jennifer Corson yesterday, and that was probably enough. I guess Paul even told him that I was the one who had asked about her, and that I heard the name from you."

"What does he want with us?"

"He only said—let's see, something about 'it's all gone on too long,' and 'everything will be straightened out.' I don't remember the exact words."

"Does he know that we—that Paul suspects something about the deaths?"

Roslyn shook her head. "I don't think so. He wouldn't be inviting us up there so openly if he did. Or I don't *think* he would be." Roslyn looked at the other woman more closely. "What do *you* think about those theories of Paul's? You didn't say much when he was talking about them today."

The dollmaker was silent. She still held the scissors and the pantyhose she had been working on. Her fingers worked the scissor blades back and forth, slowly cutting the air.

"I don't know," she said finally. "I'd never thought of something like that until he suggested it." She shook her head. "But I hadn't thought of *any* of this until last week, when you came in, and even then it took me a long time to convince myself that it might be true, that you—"

She broke off and Roslyn saw her Adam's apple bob in her throat as she swallowed.

"I don't know why it should still bother me this way," Frieda Hanneman said, and there was a faint trembling in her voice. "It was twenty years ago, whatever it was that happened. Even if everything he said *is* true, it shouldn't—and I *had* forgotten about it, until last week. Maybe not really forgotten, completely, but it was pushed back where it didn't bother me any more. Until I saw the ring. And you."

Again the older woman paused, her head moving slowly back and forth, from shadow to light, from light to shadow.

"Maybe it's because Jennifer was the closest I ever came to having a child of my own, even if I did have her only a couple of months. Maybe if Frank and I had ever— And I didn't *have* Jennifer, even those two months, not really. The only reason I had her at all was that Ruth had left her with me that day, to baby-sit. As soon as all the vultures gathered, and realized that Sophie wasn't in any shape to take the child, not right away at least—as soon as they realized they could get an inside track on Sophie's money by baby-sitting for a few months, until Sophie herself recovered enough to take Jennifer, then *everyone* wanted her. But not for herself. Not for herself . . . But we got along just fine, Jennifer and me. We got along just fine."

As Mrs. Hanneman spoke, her eyes seemed to retreat into the past until they were blank and glazed. Watching her, trying to be objective, Roslyn couldn't help but wonder if it had not been that very shortness of time that had made the attachment to the child—to Roslyn herself?—seem so great. The briefness, and the tragedies that had marked both the beginning and the ending of the period.

Like the brief and tragic love affairs that movie and TV scriptwriters presented so often, and that young girls less levelheaded than Roslyn liked to fantasize about, the memory of the two months with Jennifer was probably much more beautiful than the actual two months themselves had been.

But memories, inaccurate or not, were all that existed now, and everything she and Mrs. Hanneman did would have to be based on them. Logical reconstructions of how things must have actually been were irrelevant.

Roslyn wasn't sure how long they had spent in the silent semidarkness when a sharp rapping on the back door brought them both abruptly back to the present. Mrs. Hanneman, still blinking away the memories, walked to the door and opened it. An instant later, Benjamin Blassingrame pushed his way past her into the room.

CHAPTER 20

Mrs. Hanneman stepped back, her hand flying involuntarily toward her mouth, and Roslyn stifled a gasp.

Now I've done it, Roslyn thought, me and my big mouth. Aloud, she said: "Mr. Blassingrame, I thought we were going to meet you at your house."

He looked around the room, and even in the dim light that reached him, Roslyn could see the grimness in his lined, square face.

"Is Paul here?"

"No," Roslyn said quickly. "What made you think—"

"I know he's supposed to meet you here."

"Well, he's not here yet."

"It's just as well." Some of the tiredness Roslyn had heard in his voice on the phone reappeared, as if he had been holding it back until then. His face seemed to take on extra years as he looked from Roslyn to Frieda Hanneman.

"Frieda," he said quietly, "it's been a long time, and not very pleasant, I'm afraid."

The older woman said nothing. She had backed further from the door and was now leaning against the glass-fronted cabinet containing the stacks of doll parts.

"If it's any consolation," Blassingrame went on, "it hasn't been very pleasant for any of us."

He turned toward Roslyn again, and silently, his eyes traveled over her face. Then, for just an instant, he closed them, and he said: "You do look very much like your mother."

The silence seemed to fill the room, and Roslyn could hear her own breathing.

"My—mother?" The words came out slowly, reluctantly.

"Your mother. Ruth Corson. Ruth Blassingrame." His voice was equally soft then.

Roslyn blinked, and something that felt like a giant hand twisted at her stomach, leaving a leaden numbness behind. So now it was official. No more secondhand guesses or speculations. Here was the man who knew the truth, and he had said yes, you are not really the person you have always known you were. You are not Roslyn Stratton.

Roslyn Stratton is—

"So it's true," she said.

Blassingrame nodded and his shoulders slumped minutely as he did. "It's true," he said, and then he looked at his watch. "We had better be going."

"To your house?"

"Yes. It will be better there."

Roslyn pulled in a deep breath, trying to stop the shaking she knew would be in her voice. "I think we had better wait for Paul."

Blassingrame shook his head, and the tiredness in his face seemed to grow even deeper. "No, it will be better if we don't. If we can settle it all without his—without his help."

Again Roslyn pulled in her breath. "Just what is it you want, Mr. Blassingrame?"

"Yes," a new voice said in a speculative tone, "just what *do* you want, Dad?"

Ben Blassingrame spun around sharply toward the darkened doorway, and Roslyn's and Mrs. Hanneman's eyes jerked toward it as well. Relief, painful in its suddenness, stabbed through Roslyn as she saw Paul stepping into the room. For the first time that Roslyn could remember, Paul was not dressed in mod style or bright colors. Instead, he had on dark, almost black slacks and a shirt and zipper jacket nearly as dark. A cap, jammed down over his normally studiously disarrayed hair, shadowed his face.

Paul stood inside the door for a second, facing his father. It was hard to tell in the shadows, but there seemed to be a faint smile on Paul's face.

"Did you come to help, Dad?" he asked, then turned from his father and closed and latched the door.

"Well?" Paul asked again, as he turned back from the door and moved casually across the room to the window and lowered the shade. "*Did* you come to help?"

"Paul, what are you—" Roslyn began, but Ben waved her to silence, not imperiously but pleadingly.

"Yes," Blassingrame said finally, "I'm here to help you. You may not believe it, but I am."

Paul's smile, faint as it had been, faded and twisted. "You haven't come to your senses, then?"

"Yes, I have. After all these years, I've finally come to my senses."

Paul laughed harshly. "*Your* kind of sense, I suppose you mean? From the sanctimonious tone of your voice, that must be what you mean. Am I right?"

Blassingrame nodded. Even in the shadows, Roslyn could see the pain in his eyes. "You're actually planning to go through with it?"

"Of course," Paul said. "Did you ever think I wouldn't?"

Blassingrame's voice was almost a sob. "I hoped. God, how I hoped!"

Another harsh, derisive laugh exploded from Paul. "I'll just bet you did. And I'll also bet that's *all* you did! Just hoped! And waited for something to fall into your lap!"

Frieda Hanneman had moved backward again, along the row of cabinets and shelves to stand at the same end of the table as Roslyn. They both watched Paul and his father and listened to the suddenly surrealistic exchange with growing terror.

"Paul," Roslyn began, "what is going on? Why—"

Paul turned toward her, his face still partially shadowed. She couldn't be sure if there was a touch of sadness in his expression or not.

"I'm sorry, Roslyn," he said, "I really am. You should have given in to your sudden attack of 'homesickness' yesterday. It would have—" He stopped, shaking his head. "No, that's not quite right, either. If you had, then you wouldn't have still wanted to meet Sophie, and Dad wouldn't have broken down and told me the truth so I could help keep you away from her. And if I hadn't learned the truth in time . . ."

He shrugged. "And you"—his eyes darted toward Frieda Hanneman—"you would have still been a threat. No, Roslyn, once you came to Fowler, it was just as well it worked out the way it did. It clears everything up, gets rid of all the loose ends relatively neatly."

Ben, still near the door, a dozen feet from Paul, took a single step toward him. "Do you realize what you're saying? You're talking about human lives! Human lives!"

Again the harsh, humorless laugh, brief and explosive and frightening. "You know, Dad," Paul said in a tone that was conversational except for a trace of brittle stiffness, "for a while there, when you first told me what you had done twenty years ago, I started to have a little respect for you. I really did. Don't spoil it now. Don't ruin it completely."

"Ruin it? Didn't you understand a thing I said?"

Paul waved a hand as if to erase the words from the air. "I understood. But I *don't* understand *you*. You're willing to—now are you here to help me? Or to try to stop me?"

"Do you have to ask?" Ben moved another step forward.

Paul shook his head slowly. "No, I suppose I don't. I suppose I don't." Just as slowly, as if he had all the time in the world, he reached into one of the pockets of his jacket. When his hand emerged, a dark shape glinted there in the faint light.

Frieda Hanneman gasped and leaned heavily against the table. Roslyn stared unbelievingly. "Paul, I don't understand—"

He glanced toward her but kept the gun—the same one he had offered her for protection, she wondered?—trained on his father. "Are you sure you don't understand, Ros? It's quite simple," he said. "No matter what my father says, I have no intention of taking a chance on losing everything."

"But you *wouldn't*," his father said, a note of desperation entering his voice. "I'm sure they would be reasonable. *Wouldn't* you?" He turned toward the two women pleadingly.

"I'm sure they would—now," Paul said, a rising amusement in his voice. "After all, what would they have to lose by promising to be—'reasonable'? Was that the word you used? But once we're away from here, once they're out of reach, what's to stop them from becoming most unreasonable?"

He shook his head. "No, this is the only way. I'm really surprised you don't see it. The one remaining question is, how many 'loose ends' do we have? Two? Or three?"

The older man stared at his son in silence. Ben's jaw trembled slightly, and the tendons in his neck stood out as he fought to hold himself steady. He took another step toward Paul.

"Give me the gun, Paul."

Paul stared at him blankly for a moment. The gun, as if it had a life of its own, raised slightly, steadied itself.

"Give it to me." Ben's voice was steady now, flat, almost like an automaton's. He took another step.

Paul shook his head. "Your last chance, Father Benjamin," he said steadily, but there was a slight widening of his eyes as he eased himself backward a fraction. "There's no danger involved, you know that. If *you* don't talk, there's nothing to connect either of us with this. And Horace can certainly control *his* son, at least enough to keep any investigation low key. If you tell him to . . ."

Paul backed away another step as Ben moved another step forward. The gun remained steady.

"I don't understand you," Paul went on, his voice tighter now. "After what you did, are you willing to throw it all away now? For two people you hardly know? I can't believe it!"

"I know you can't. And that's the most terrible thing of all, knowing that, somehow, I must be responsible for that. I raised you, so I must be responsible. But I won't be responsible for allowing you to—"

"I said stop!" Paul slid backward another pace.

Ben continued forward, his eyes now fastened to his son's as if trying to open some kind of communication with him through sheer intensity of will. He took another step forward and held his right hand out, palm up.

"Give it to me, son, and we'll forget this whole—"

A flash of fire in the shadows and a deafening crack in the enclosed space of the room, and Ben Blassingrame reeled backward, stumbling, clutching at his right arm. The arm dangled limply as he half fell against the table a few feet from where the kiln stood. The table shook under the impact and the kiln wobbled for an instant but settled back.

Frieda Hanneman, her mouth open but not screaming, stood rigid and unmoving, and Roslyn, in an automatic action, started toward Ben Blassingrame.

"Stay back!" Paul's voice was even harsher than before, almost grating, and Roslyn stopped abruptly, teetering on the balls of her feet, one hand out to steady herself against the table.

"I didn't want to do that," Paul said, his voice quieter, his eyes shifting toward his father, "I really didn't. You can still come over to my—" He stopped, seeming to choke on the words.

"No," he said abruptly, his voice once again becoming almost conversational with only a slight tension evident in the clipped way the words came out. "No, you can't. I should know that by now. It wouldn't work. You've made yourself into another loose end—the biggest loose end of all." He laughed, but much of the harshness was gone, as if, now that he knew what he had to do, he was more in control of himself. There was, Roslyn thought, even a touch of amusement in the laugh. "You and 'Miss Stratton' and Horace's kid," he went on, "you're all the same when you get to the bottom line. Dedicated. You can't give up, not for your life." Another laugh. "Not even for your life."

He motioned with the gun. "All right, all three of you move around behind the table, back by the door to the basement." He glanced toward Ben, who was leaning heavily on the table edge, supporting himself with his left arm. "Give him a hand if you want to."

Roslyn moved to the wounded man and half supported him as he put his left arm across her shoulders. His eyes were dull with shock and he moved slowly. Blood had already formed a dark pool on the floor at his feet, and Roslyn could hear the steady drip as they moved around the table. She thought of leaping for the door as they passed within a half dozen feet of it, but she knew that by the time she worked the latch it would be far too late. The numbness that had been confined to her stomach before now seemed to have spread throughout her entire body, and she felt as if she were walking in her sleep. Surely, she thought, she would wake up any second now. Surely . . .

As Paul shepherded them around the table toward the basement door, he moved closer to the kiln. He held his empty hand out toward it, then pulled back and smiled.

"I'd like to thank you," he said, "for making it all so easy, getting this all heated up for me." He glanced around at the shadowy shelves and cabinets. "I don't suppose you'd like to go even further and tell me which of your cans and jugs there would be the most inflammable? No, I didn't think you would."

He shrugged. "Well, I do like there to be some small challenge in things, even this. Once you're locked away downstairs, I'm sure that I'll be able to find something among your glues and waxes and the rest that will serve my purpose admirably. A small spill next to this thing should serve quite well, don't you think?"

He glanced toward the kiln again. "I'm really surprised you haven't had a fire here before, as hot as that thing gets. Even the outside must be quite hot enough to start a good blaze, provided I find the right starter material."

He stopped and looked more closely at the kiln, at the closed peephole in the center of the door. "Incidentally, what are you making in there?"

Suddenly, a faint hope blossomed deep inside Roslyn, a small tingling thing, insubstantial and improbable. There had been a line in one of the ceramics books she had looked through at the library the week before, a warning. A warning that had said . . .

"A doll," Roslyn said, keeping her voice dull and flat despite the growing tingle inside her. She glanced toward Frieda Hanneman. "She was duplicating the doll that started this whole trouble. From what I've seen, it's a very good likeness."

Paul frowned thoughtfully. "And since that box is built to withstand all kinds of temperatures, I suppose the doll would survive the fire."

Roslyn nodded.

"That would be just a little inconvenient," Paul mused. "Not very, but just a little. Probably nothing would ever come of it—unless someone from the *Journal* decided to print a picture of the 'last item the deceased was working on.' Not likely, but still a possibility . . ."

He glanced around the room again, careful to keep the gun leveled at the three of them. "I think you said this afternoon you had asbestos gloves somewhere? I don't suppose you would—but never mind, I see them."

He moved to a shelf, and with his free hand, took down one of the gloves. Keeping the gun leveled at the three of them, he worked the glove onto his left hand and moved back toward the kiln.

"That's what turns it off, there at the bottom?" He reached out and turned the multiple-position switch. A moment later the small red light to the left of the switch went out.

"Anything special about opening the door?" he asked. "But then, I don't imagine you would tell me if there was." He seemed to be enjoying himself now, as if it were a parlor game of some kind. And perhaps to him, Roslyn thought, it was.

He moved a little to one side so that the kiln would not be between his gun and the three of them when he pulled the door open. He leaned down slightly. The handle looked simple enough, and he reached for it and pulled tentatively. He could feel the warmth even through the glove. There was a slight snap as a catch released, and the door opened a crack. His eyes alternating between the kiln door and the three people under his gun, he leaned further down, and with a smooth motion, pulled the door open.

Suddenly, there was a cracking like a rifle shot.

Paul half fell, half leaped backward, his hands flying to his face, a shrill scream erupting from his throat. As he smashed into the cabinet next to the door, the gun flew from his hand, clattering against the pegboards on the wall to his right.

Roslyn, who had eased Ben's arm from her shoulder as she had stood waiting, darted forward, forcing herself to act, not think. Her heart was pounding, and during the seconds that she had been tensed, waiting and hoping desperately for the explosion that finally came when the cold air from the room touched the two-thousand-degree clay, the sides of her blouse had become soaked with cold, icy sweat.

The gun hit the pegboard and seemed to stick for an instant on one of the pegs, then bounced and clattered downward like a mis-shapen ball in a huge pinball machine. As it hit the floor Roslyn, half falling, half diving, lunged for it, her hands reaching and scrabbling in the shadows.

Then she had it, her fingers tightening around the barrel, and she scrambled backward, afraid to look up. Trying to get her feet under her and still hold onto the gun, she reeled backward until she fell sideways and slammed against the basement door.

Finally, she looked up, still fumbling to get the gun pointed in the right direction.

But it was unnecessary, she saw immediately. Paul, his hands dropped to his sides now, was slumped back against the cabinet he had crashed into, the glass in one of the doors cracked. A half dozen spots on his face, one almost touching his left eye, were dead white, seared dry. On his left cheek, a half inch from the edge of his mouth, a small jagged piece of fired clay still stuck, and Roslyn could see a tendril of smoke rising leisurely. As she watched, the fragment fell away, revealing the same dead white of the other half dozen burns. Then, as if a miniature tide was rising within his body, the areas around the spots began to redden and flush as the blood rushed in.

His arms trembled as he fought to keep his hands from grasping at the seared spots of flesh, and his lips moved feebly.

"A doctor." The words emerged slowly, painfully. "Find a doctor . . ."

His arms still stiff and trembling at his sides, Paul Blassingrame slid unevenly down the front of the cabinet to the floor.

CHAPTER 21

As Eric Macklin turned the car between the stone pillars and started up the long, curving driveway, Roslyn could hear, faint and distant, the buzz of a power mower somewhere on the immaculately kept Blassingrame grounds. Probably the last cutting of the season, she thought, as she looked out at the tinges of brown and orange that were beginning to speckle the dozens of oaks and elms scattered between the house and the road. As the car slowed, Roslyn lowered the window an inch or two, letting in the crisp, autumn air.

She looked up at the huge house, two massive stories that seemed to stretch out interminably from either side of the outsize front door that only now was coming into sight fifty yards away.

"Stop here," she said, not completely sure why she spoke.

Eric glanced sideways at her, and the car slid smoothly to a stop at the edge of the drive.

"Nerves?" he asked.

She nodded, wriggled back into the seat cushions. "Something like that. It's not every day you meet an incredibly rich grandmother you didn't know you had until two days ago." She forced a small laugh. "The library doesn't have any books that cover the protocol for situations like this."

"Not much call for it, I imagine."

"No, probably not. I doubt that I'll ever need it myself after today."

They sat silently for a minute, and then Eric reached over and took her hand lightly. She glanced toward him, a quick, nervous smile crossing her face. She squeezed his hand.

She looked toward the house again. On the right side, just visible beyond the house, she could see the mower she had heard before. A riding mower, she thought, of course.

"I wonder what they'll do with Paul?" Even as she spoke, she knew she wasn't asking for information. She was just talking to keep from having to go the last fifty yards to the house. She wished now that she had been more insistent that they wait until she could have gone back to Wisconsin to explain everything to her mother— her *real* mother, no matter what the biological facts were—and maybe even gotten her to come back to Fowler with her. She would come eventually, Roslyn was sure, but . . .

"That will be up to Sophie," Eric was saying, "and Ben. And you, for that matter. But there's plenty of time to worry about that when they let him out of the hospital."

"Will they be able to save his eye?"

"They don't know yet. They have hopes, but it will be close. Dad called in the best eye man in the state, so if they don't make it, it won't be for lack of trying."

Roslyn was silent again, her eyes once more drifting across the front of the house and the acres of grounds.

"You know," she said, "no matter what he tried to do to us, I still can't help but feel sorry for him, just a little." She looked toward Eric. "I saw him in the hospital yesterday, but he wouldn't even talk to me. They said he hadn't spoken more than a half dozen words to anyone since he was brought in."

Eric nodded. "I can't say I feel sorry for him, but . . . I don't think it's the injury that's got him down, or even the possibility that he'll go to jail—although I doubt that he ever will. It's just the realization that his free ride is over. Once he gets out of this, he'll be just another mortal, maybe in worse shape than most of us."

"And your father? How's he taking it?"

Eric smiled. "He's glad as hell it's all over. He got a full night's sleep last night for just about the first time in twenty years, he said."

"He won't have to give up his practice, will he?"

Eric's face turned sober. "I don't know. Again, that's up to you and your mother. And a few other people. I think he almost hopes they will take his license away. In fact, if Ben hadn't talked him out of it a half dozen times, Dad would have confessed the whole thing long ago. Especially when he saw what sort of person Paul was turning into. But I guess Ben kept convincing him to keep it quiet just a little longer."

He shrugged. "And I think Ben kept convincing himself, too. Deep down, he knew what Paul was. He bought him out of enough scrapes, bought off enough girls over the years, but he just wouldn't admit it to himself. He couldn't believe that the son he had gone so far out on the limb for twenty years ago could turn out so bad. Even that last night, when he and my father convinced me it was for your own good that I let them know where you were supposed to meet me and Paul—even then, when Ben knew, inside, what Paul was planning, he wouldn't admit it. He still thought that if he went there by himself, he could talk Paul out of it."

Eric stopped, shaking his head slowly, the fingers of his left hand working the steering wheel back and forth a fraction of an inch.

"What about Ben?" Roslyn knew the answer, but she asked the question anyway. "He didn't do any of the things—the killings—that Paul said. He never actually harmed anyone directly. Not seriously. Whatever it was he had your father give me at the party, and the other thing Tuesday—what was that, anyway?"

"I don't know. Dad gave it a name, but it was medical jargon, not legal jargon, so it didn't stick. Some variety of barbiturate. He just gave you a quick piece of narcotherapy so he could plant a post-hypnotic suggestion for you to be homesick as hell." A faint smile returned to his face. "He apologized profusely and said he just hadn't counted on your subconscious still hanging onto memories from the time you lived at the cottage."

"Yes, the 'homesickness' did seem to vanish the instant I got back there. The way it disappeared so fast, though, scared me almost as much as all the strange feelings it had been giving me before. I really thought for a minute I was going off the deep end for sure. But it didn't really hurt anything. Neither of those things did."

She shook her head and looked around still another time. "I've never been good at this kind of decision, where I have to hand out guilt or innocence. It'd be so damn much easier in a movie. Inherit the fortune and live happily ever after and send the miscreants responsible for the mess to jail."

She looked back at Eric, her hand involuntarily closing more tightly on his. "But damn it! I don't want to send anyone to jail! Hell, I can't even decide whether anybody really got hurt in this whole thing besides Ben and your father—and maybe Paul. Who knows, if he hadn't had everything given to him so easily, he might have turned out differently."

"Don't forget Frieda Hanneman," Eric said quietly, "and Sophie."

Roslyn was silent for several seconds. "And don't forget my mother, either. She gained as much as either of them lost."

Eric nodded, sighing. "You're being remarkably charitable."

"Am I? Not really. It's called confusion, not charity. That's the trouble with something like this. It's all so damned speculative. There's practically nothing that's certain. For anyone. Would Paul have turned out differently? Or Carl and Vivian? All I know is, my parents had a daughter they wouldn't have had otherwise. And I had a good family. Not rich, maybe, but at least as good as any of the Blassingrames. Sophie included."

She shook her head again. "No, it's just confusion, not charity. I know I should probably be angry and outraged, but I'm not. And don't ask me why. I don't know."

Eric smiled faintly. "If I ever get back into law and start doing trial work, I want you on all my juries." He looked toward the house. The door was opening and Ben Blassingrame, his arm bandaged and supported by a sling, was looking out.

"Ready?" Eric asked. "Ready to go in and meet your new grandmother?"

Roslyn shuddered. "No, but I guess we had better get started. The sooner we get going, the sooner it will be over."

Eric's eyes met hers for a moment. "You're *sure* you want me with you in there?"

She nodded emphatically. "You're damned right I do!"

Eric chuckled lightly and gave her hand a final squeeze before releasing it. As the car moved forward, covering the last fifty yards to the door where Ben Blassingrame waited, his head lowered, she pulled in a deep breath, steeling herself for what was to come.

Then she looked out of the corner of her eye toward Eric and murmured, so softly she wasn't sure if he heard her or not: "After all, we dedicated types have to stick together."